D0057075

WITHDRAWN

THE SWAG IS IN THE SOCKS

ALSO BY KELLY J. BAPTIST

Isaiah Dunn Is My Hero

THE SWAG IS IN THE SOCKS

KELLY J. BAPTIST

Crown Books for Young Readers

New York

Text copyright © 2021 by Kelly J. Baptist
Jacket art and interior illustrations copyright © 2021 by Shannon Wright

Visit us on the Web! rhcbooks.com

Educators and librarians, for a variety of teaching tools, visit us at
RHTeachersLibrarians.com

Library of Congress Cataloging-in-Publication Data
Names: Baptist, Kelly J., author.
Title: The swag is in the socks / Kelly J. Baptist.
Description: First edition. | New York: Crown Books for Young Readers, [2021] |
Audience: Ages 8–12. | Audience: Grades 4–6. | Summary:
Twelve-year-old Xavier Moon gets the courage to step out of the shadows when his great-uncle gives him some outlandish socks and some even stranger requests.
Identifiers: LCCN 2021018812 (print) | LCCN 2021018813 (ebook) |
ISBN 978-0-593-38086-4 (hardcover) | ISBN 978-0-593-38087-1 (library binding) |
ISBN 978-0-593-38088-8 (ebook)
Subjects: CYAC: Great-uncles–Fiction. | Socks–Fiction. | Stuttering–Fiction. |
Self-confidence–Fiction. | African Americans–Fiction. | Middle schools–Fiction. |
Schools–Fiction.
Classification: LCC PZ7.1.B3674 Sw 2021 (print) | LCC PZ7.1.B3674 (ebook) |
DDC [Fic]–dc23

The text of this book is set in 11.5-point Gamma ITC Std. Book.
Interior design by Cathy Bobak

Printed in the United States of America
10 9 8 7 6 5 4 3 2 1
First Edition

For my big sister, Kim, who helps kids find their words and their voice; Frankie McGinnis, a master of the keys; and Mr. Roseburgh, middle school principal by day, Kappa for life!

Scepter League Creed

I am a young man of purpose,

A descendant of kings.

As a member of the illustrious Scepter League,

I am disciplined, courageous, and confident.

I will carry myself with dignity and honor

in all situations.

I will respect myself, my family,

My school, and my community.

I will be academically excellent,

Physically fit,

And socially responsible.

I will be a man who lights the way for others.

CHAPTER 1

*"There's nothing too spectacular
about you."*

"Well, jack my phone and call me Jill; that fool done it again!"

Aunt Kat shuffles into the living room and lowers herself into her special peach-colored easy chair, a piece of paper in her hand and a frown on her face. She tosses the paper onto the coffee table in front of her. Me and my sister, Shannon, call it the Obama Table, since Aunt Kat's got practically every magazine he was ever on the cover of.

Shannon's in the kitchen, chopping the life outta something, and she calls over, "What's wrong, Aunt Kat?"

Aunt Kat shakes her head, the corners of her mouth turned down like she just smelled one of my power-farts.

"Cain't even speak on it, girl," she says at first, which only means she's gonna speak on it in 5 . . . 4 . . . 3 . . . 2 . . .

"But that fool brother of mine done took off again to God knows where!"

"You think he's okay?" Shannon asks.

"Pffft!" Aunt Kat makes a loud noise with her lips. "Who gonna know that? For all I know, he's somewhere slumped over a piano havin' a heart attack, while some used-to-be singer tries to hold on to her note *and* her wig!"

I bust out laughing before I can stop myself. I shut my mouth real quick and try to go back to being invisible on the couch, praying Aunt Kat don't look my way and tell me my ten minutes on the Nintendo Switch are up. I know, right? Who gives a ten-minute video game limit?

Aunt Kat.

Luckily, she's too upset about her brother leaving to pay any attention to me. She mutters about how ungrateful he is, and who's gonna pay his part of the bills here at the house now that he's gone. Not gonna lie; Frankie Bell always gets the good groceries when he's home.

It's really not a shocker, but Aunt Kat's actin' like this has never happened before. To be honest, this happens almost every month! Her brother, my great-uncle, Frankie Bell, is a musician—a piano player—and according to him, he's been playing since birth, and traveling as much as he can with his group, the Bell-Aires.

"I started off strumming the umbilical cord," Frankie Bell tells anybody who asks. "But when I got out that womb prison, it was all about the keys."

Frankie Bell's been in bands since he was fifteen, and he says he'll be in one till they're playing for his funeral.

Aunt Kat, who's technically my *great*-aunt, was the oldest of six kids, and all that's left is her and Frankie Bell, the youngest. My grandfather, who was next in line after Aunt Kat, died when I was three. All I remember about him is the smell of Vicks VapoRub and cigar smoke. So Frankie Bell, which is what everybody calls him, is the closest thing to a grandfather I got. He's cool but kinda weird. Aunt Kat says he's ten steps past crazy, whatever that means.

"You watch," Aunt Kat says, pointing at his letter. "Whenever he goes on the road for a long time, he starts sending letters that don't make a lick of sense! He picks some poor soul to torment with his secret instructions and whatnot, like he's the wisest man to draw a breath. Messes with their minds so much, they start thinkin' *they* the ones losing it!"

Aunt Kat cusses and Shannon looks up all shocked.

"Ooooh, Aunt Kat!" she says, but I can tell she's tryin' not to laugh. I am, too. I keep it in this time.

"I'm sorry, baby, but that's what Frankie Bell is full of."

Shannon opens the oven, and a whoosh of good smells floats out.

"How long 'fore we can eat?" Aunt Kat asks, noticing the smell, too.

" 'Bout fifteen minutes," Shannon says. She picks up her cell phone and sends a text. I bet anything it's to Julian.

She claims Ju's her "friend," but we all know better. Aunt Kat hates him, thinks he's too old for Shannon cuz he's eighteen and she just turned sixteen. I don't think it's that big of a deal, especially since Ju's one of them dudes who's got everything going for him: star quarterback, girls are obsessed with him, *and* he's smart. He says he's gonna be an anesthesiologist, but even that doesn't win Aunt Kat over. She says he could be the next Black Jesus, but something about him still don't sit right with her.

It's probably his teeth, which, to me, are his only flaw. Two on the bottom are kinda crooked, like they're tryin' to high-five each other. This obviously doesn't bother Shannon, but teeth are definitely a "thing" for Aunt Kat. "Crooked teeth, crooked feet" (whatever *that* means) is what she told me when she forced me to get braces a year ago.

The best thing about Ju is that he's in the Scepter

League, which is a *huge* deal. It's this club that was started at Rosewood Public Schools, like, a hundred years ago. You gotta have super swag to get in, and if you do, you become kinda famous around the city. At my school, dudes in the Scepter League are like kings. Once a month, they wear their blazers and ties and get to skip the line at lunch and miss last hour to have important meetings in the library with teachers and the principal. Sometimes they even go over to the high school to link with the Leaguers there. They get a section reserved for them in the gym during basketball games, and Rosewood games *always* be sold out. Once they're old enough to get jobs, Scepter Leaguers work at the rec center, or the bank, or at the stadium downtown—never at some greasy fast-food place. And the girls? Maaaan, if you're in the Scepter League, it's pretty much a guarantee that they notice you. My #goals for seventh grade? Get in.

"Xavier, you still on that game machine?" Aunt Kat asks, not even looking at me. Dang, I thought she was all into this judge show she just turned on. Guess not.

"No," I say, turning the Switch off.

"Good! That mess is rotting your brain, one cell at a time," she says. "Why somebody would willingly buy that, I do not know."

I swallow hard and slide the Switch into my pocket.

I love Aunt Kat and all, but sometimes she goes too far. My dad gave me the Switch before he got locked up, and no matter how she feels about it, it's special.

I walk to the kitchen to peek at the birthday cake that's chillin' on the counter. Double chocolate, just like I asked, with *Happy 12th Birthday, Xavier!* written across the top in fancy green cursive. I open the freezer: pistachio ice cream, check!

"Get out the kitchen, Xavier, it's almost ready," fusses Shannon. She always gets moody when Ju takes too long to respond to her texts. I slide my finger across the cake for a nice taste of the icing. Shannon's too busy staring at her phone to notice.

I told her I just wanted pizza, but no, she had to go all fancy, said a birthday dinner can't be just some pizza. It smells so good in here, I *almost* agree with her. Only problem is, it took, like, *all* afternoon to make, and I'm starvin'! Pizza's much quicker, I'm just sayin'.

Shannon's been into food since before she was tall enough to see over the stove. I'm the one who has to try all her "creations," and she still hogs the TV watching the Food Network. Guess I can't complain too much, though, cuz my b-day dinner is Cajun chicken linguine. Add in some sautéed asparagus with Shannon's signature lemon butter sauce, a salad, and homemade garlic bread, and I got a five-star meal.

"Okay, let's just eat," Shannon says a few minutes later. Guess Ju hasn't called or texted, cuz she looks like she wants to smack somebody.

"'Bout time," Aunt Kat mutters, pulling herself up from her easy chair. "Boy gonna be thirteen by the time we sit down."

Shannon's got the table set all fancy—no paper plates—and in the middle is a pitcher of my all-time favorite drink: strawberry lemonade mixed with cherry 7UP. Yo, I won't say this out loud, but I got a pretty good sis.

"Aunt Kat, you gonna pray for the food?" Shannon asks, which is this joke we have.

"And get struck down before I can eat? Hell, no!" Aunt Kat says. Me and Shannon grin, and Shannon blesses the food. She barely says amen when we hear footsteps on the porch and three quick knocks.

Julian.

"Yo, sorry I'm late, everybody," he says with a crooked-tooth grin. He goes to side-hug Aunt Kat, and she has a stank look on her face the whole time.

"Hmmph!"

"Happy birthday, bro!" Ju tells me, giving me dap and dropping a ten-dollar Taco Bell gift card on the table by my plate.

"Thanks," I say, kinda shocked that he actually got me something.

Ju takes off his green-and-gold Scepter League jacket, which he wears even more than his football letter jacket. He sits across from me and piles his plate high with linguine while my eyes lock onto that jacket like a magnet, imagining my name in bold lettering on the front of one . . . soon.

"This smells sooo good, Shan," he says, shoveling a huge bite into his mouth.

Shannon's attitude is gone now that Ju is here, and she actually grins and *sighs*, like everything is all good now. Ridiculous, right?

"So how it feel to be twelve?" asks Ju, crunching on the garlic bread. "Exact same as eleven, right?"

I nod. He's pretty much got it. No magic feeling when I woke up today.

"Hope you like the food, Xav," Shannon says, "cuz that's the only present you gonna get from me."

I shake my head and take a giant bite of the linguine.

"You gonna do this for *my* birthday?" Ju asks, reaching for another piece of garlic bread.

Aunt Kat opens her mouth to say something else, probably something about Ju being too old for Shannon anyway, but then we hear more footsteps on the porch, followed by the half-working doorbell.

"Now, who in creation is that?" Aunt Kat asks with a frown. "You expecting somebody else, Shannon?"

"No," Shannon says, a confused frown on her face, too.

"You got your hooligan friends coming to my house?" Aunt Kat narrows her eyes and points her fork at Ju.

"No, ma'am," Ju says quickly.

"I'll go see who—" Shannon starts to say, but then Aunt Kat holds up her hand and cuts her off.

"Ah Lord," she mutters. "I already know who that is." It takes the rest of us a few seconds of listening before we know, too.

Shannon goes to the door, and before any of us are ready, my mother's sisters crash my dinner.

Aunt Nadine's the oldest, super bossy and loud. Surprised she drove all the way from Chesterfield, a suburb that's over an hour away. Aunt Crystal is next. She's a tad nicer than Aunt Nadine, but just as loud.

"Happy birthday, baby!" Aunt Nadine shouts the second she sees me. She waltzes by Aunt Kat to hug me and give me an oversized kiss on the cheek. "Look at you, the Big Twelve and all! Twins, say happy birthday to your cousin!"

Great. I didn't notice Stephen and Stacy slink in behind the aunts. They're ten, but already too much like their mom, which means they act like they better than everybody else.

"Happy birthday," they say at the same time, like they're bored out their minds. Stacy literally yawns as she looks around the dining room, probably critiquing how *poor* we are compared to them.

"Can't believe you're twelve!" Aunt Crys says, hugging and kissing me next. She ties a bunch of balloons around my chair, like I'm four or something. There's an awkward silence until Shannon asks if they wanna make plates. Yeah, she's only sixteen, but she's pretty motherly, always making sure people are comfortable.

"Oh, *no*, sweetie," Aunt Nadine says. "We're gluten-free, you know."

"Sense-free, too," Aunt Kat mutters.

I always thought it was scary how Aunt Nadine can have a smile on her face while looking at something (or someone) like it's the most disgusting thing in the world. That's how she's looking at Shannon's food, and it's making me mad.

"I'll take a plate," Aunt Crys says. Trying to be the peacemaker, I guess. She fixes a tiny bit of everything and sits next to me.

"You guys remember Ju, right?" Shannon says, cuz clearly, there ain't much else to say.

"Yes, how are you, Ju?" Aunt Crys says.

"Pretty good, thanks," Ju tells her.

"What is that short for again? Justice? Juvontay?" Aunt Nadine asks, wrinkling her nose.

Aunt Kat snorts. "Now, you know damn well—"

"Um, it's actually Julian," Ju says.

"Hmmm." Aunt Nadine's word hangs in the air like rotten skunk spray.

"And you guys go to the same school?" asks Aunt Crys.

"Yeah," Shannon says. She side-eyes Aunt Kat, who would usually throw in some kind of snarky comment about their grade difference. But I think since Aunt Kat can't stand Nadine and Crys, Ju's off the hook this time.

"That's nice," Aunt Crys says, fake-smiling. She takes a few more bites of linguine. "This is really good, Shannon."

"Thanks," Shannon says. "You ready for cake, Xav?"

I nod. My plate is clean, and I was thinkin' about seconds, but I can always do that later.

Ju helps Shannon clear the table and then they return with my cake, all lit up with candles. Can't help but smile while they sing "Happy Birthday," especially since they sound horrible. I get all the candles out in one try, and when Shannon hands me the knife, I make sure everybody gets huge hunks. Everybody who wants a piece, that is. Stephen and Stacy stand by the wall the whole time, but I swear I can see drool comin' out their mouths as me, Shannon, Ju, and Aunt Kat attack our pieces.

"Ready for school to start, Xavier?" Aunt Nadine asks, continuing without giving me a chance to answer. "The twins are beyond excited. It'll be such a busy year for them!"

Aunt Nadine rambles on and on about their violin lessons, and tennis, and how they might be picked for a modeling campaign. I tune her out and think about what *my* year's gonna be like. Most people think seventh grade ain't all that important. It's not like sixth grade, when you're just starting middle school, or eighth grade, with all the class trips and the moving-on ceremony. But at Rosewood, seventh grade means I'm eligible for the Scepter League. *Finally!*

I look over at Stephen. Poor dude. I bet Aunt Nadine would never let him go out for the League. The twins are like her little puppets! I feel sorry for them, having to listen to her go on and on and on all the time.

All of a sudden, Aunt Nadine stops talking and looks dead at me, like she just read my thoughts. I almost choke on a glob of chocolate icing!

"Have you heard from your mother today, Xavier?"

The room goes casket quiet, except for the sound of Shannon's fork dropping onto her empty plate, and Aunt Crys hissing "Nadine!" a few seconds later.

My mother—*our* mother—is Shay Elyse Bell, their little sister. And Aunt Nadine asking if I've heard from her makes me so mad, I forget to stay quiet. The minute I open my mouth, though, I regret it.

"N-n-n-n-not yet. B-b-b-but I will."

Aunt Nadine wrinkles her face.

"Oh, poor baby," she says, puckering her lips and turning to Aunt Kat. "He still does that? Guess that's public-school education for you."

"Get the hell outta my house," Aunt Kat growls, standing so fast, the twins jump and inch their way toward the door.

"Aunt Kat, calm down," Shannon says, getting in between Aunt Kat and Aunt Nadine.

"We should go," Aunt Crys says. Umm, duh! She gives me a sad smile and whispers, "Happy birthday, baby."

"What?" Aunt Nadine looks truly confused. "That is a reasonable question, is it not?"

"I'm 'bout to show you reasonable," Aunt Kat says. Ju jumps up, too, but he knows better than to grab Aunt Kat's arm the way Shannon does.

"Nadine, let's go." Aunt Crys tugs her sister's other arm.

"Why, Crystal?" Aunt Nadine's voice is definitely more hood now, like she just remembered *she* went to the same public school I go to. "Why can't we ask about our sister? Hell, I was even gonna ask about her no-good man, too!"

Aunt Crys literally yanks Aunt Nadine toward the door, and it's a good thing, cuz Aunt Kat starts swinging and cussing. I stand up, but I have no idea what to do or say. My mouth opens and I wanna scream that my dad *was* here; that he woke me up early and took me out to breakfast at The Yard, where the pancakes are the size of the plate and the hot chocolate has two inches of whipped cream on top of it.

But that was four birthdays ago.

This morning, all I got from him was a two-minute phone call.

Shannon yells for me to stay where I am, and both she and Ju struggle to hold Aunt Kat back.

"Get her out!" Shannon yells at Aunt Crys. The twins are squealing, Aunt Kat's cussing up a storm, and I can't get a single word out.

I leave it all—my half-eaten hunk of chocolate cake, seconds on linguine, and my gift card from Ju—and head up the creaky stairs to my room without saying a word. I flop on my bed and turn my Switch on, volume way up. Still doesn't drown out Aunt Kat yelling things you don't expect an old lady to say. I hear doors slam, a car start, and the sound of the car screeching down the street.

Then it's quiet.

Shannon's probably trying to calm Aunt Kat so she don't have a heart attack the way my grandfather did. Rumor is, he was pissed at my mom about something she'd done and was yelling his head off when all of a sudden, he just fell over. Died on the way to the hospital. My mom tried to be tough, but she blamed herself for what happened to him, even though the doctors said his heart had been bad for years. Maybe the bad things she did after that was because of guilt.

Nobody talks about it much, and I don't know all the details, but two years, three months ago, my mom and dad did something that got them both locked up. Since my dad was really into cars, I always imagine it was some *Fast and Furious*-type stuff. What they did really doesn't matter to me; what matters is that they ain't here.

Shannon was almost fourteen then, but she figured me and her could just go on like normal, since she was already used to being my number two mom. She didn't understand why we had to leave our house and move in with Aunt Kat and sometimes-there Frankie Bell. Far as she was concerned, me and her coulda just stayed in our house on our own. I love Aunt Kat and all, but I can't wait for things to go back to normal when my parents are out.

"Xav?"

Shannon knocks on my door and peeks her head in at the same time.

"What?" I say. Cool thing about Shannon is that she'll know I'm not mad at her, just everything else.

Shannon sighs and comes all the way in, closing the door behind her.

"You okay?" she asks. "They a hot mess! You *know* none of us invited them."

I just nod.

"Aunt Kat got you stuff," Shannon says with a sigh. "You wanna come down and open your gifts? Or just chill up here?"

"Ch-chill," I tell her. I don't stutter as much around Shannon, but she's 'bout the only one. When I'm around people, I mostly keep my mouth closed or give super-short answers.

"Aight," Shannon says. She pauses a sec, then says, "I'll bring you the phone when she calls, okay?"

I nod. When Shannon leaves, I put my game down and stare at the ceiling. There's a bunch of spots up there that look like random things: a smiley face, a coffee mug, and a sock. When it's hard to go to sleep, I make myself find each thing, lose it by looking somewhere else on the ceiling, and then find it again. It's different, I know, but it always knocks me out.

Tonight, I stare at nothing. I keep waiting for the phone to ring, and when it finally does, I don't have to guess the words that are flashing across Aunt Kat's old-school caller ID: *Malcolm County Women's Correctional Facility.*

Wish it just said *Shay Bell.* Better yet, wish my parents didn't have to call to say happy birthday.

Again.

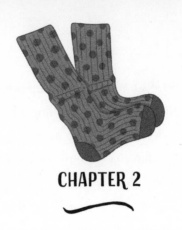

CHAPTER 2

*"It's man time, and every man needs
a trademark."*

I'm barely awake when I hear it. An annoying voice getting louder and louder.

"Xavier! XAVIER! Come outside! Hydrant's busted!"

My window's already open, and when I peek out, I immediately see Walter's big head. He's waving so hard, his whole body's shaking. Walter's nine, and probably the only dude on the planet with less swag than me. For some reason, though, he likes following me around. I think it's because he's an only child. Aunt Kat says his parents knew better than to produce The Sequel.

"You comin'?" Walter screams. Jeez, I gotta get him to shut up before Aunt Kat starts cussing at him for hollerin' outside her house. He was pretty much bawlin' last time she did that.

I give Walter a thumbs-up and he jumps up and down like he just got a new bike or something. I shake my head. Walter's a different kind of dude.

The window is the best part of my room. It's a regular window, I guess, but it's in the perfect spot to see just about all the block. Larmity Avenue always has something going on—kids playing, couples fighting, dudes washing their cars, old people planting flowers, ice cream truck getting mobbed—and I get to see it all from my room, without having to go out and talk to anyone, unless Walter is bugging me. When my parents got locked up, I didn't want to move into Aunt Kat's house, point-blank, *period.* But this window in my room makes things a little bit better. Watching the block calms me down, and I know that one day, I'll see Ma and Dad rolling into the driveway.

I throw on a T-shirt, shorts, and the raggedy sneakers I been wearing all summer. Used to be white, but now they're gray and the laces are more like brown. Aunt Kat says I can wear 'em till the soles fall off. Another one of her sayings is that the soul of the shoe is in the sole. Riiiight.

"Xavier, I hope you gonna tell that boy to shut his trap," Aunt Kat tells me as I run down the stairs. For such a loud lady, I don't see how she's got such a big problem with noise. "Yellin' to wake the dead is what he's doin'! Where in creation is his mama, letting him do all that hollerin'!"

"I g-g-got it, Aunt Kat," I say. Normally when she gets upset, she puts me to work doing random chores, so I go out onto the porch before she says anything else.

Walter's grinning all big, water dripping down his face, and he runs up and gives me a huge, wet hug.

"Yo!" I say, pushing him back when he doesn't let go right away.

"C'mon! It's down by Miz Pacey's house," he says. Miz Pacey lives near the end of Larmity, and we gotta pass a bunch of houses to get there. Walter talks to everybody he sees outside.

"Mr. Talbert! Come get in the water!" Walter yells. Mr. Talbert is this old guy who lives across the street from Walter.

"These ol' bones couldn't take it," Mr. Talbert calls. "Y'all have the fun for me!"

After Walter tells Miz Ruth her flowers look amazing, Walter points down the street and starts bouncing all over the place.

"Guess what?" Walter asks me, his mouth going a mile a minute. It's like he talks enough for both of us. "Some new people are moving in right there; see the truck? It's the green house with the brown roof and the windows that look like eyes. They're super lucky, right? They'll be so close to the playground!"

I always thought that green house was cool. It's probably the tallest on the block, and the attic windows do kinda look like eyes. Seeing the moving truck gets me thinking about where we'll live when my parents get out. Maybe it can be right here on Larmity.

When me and Walter get closer to the busted fire hydrant, he takes off running and screaming into the water. A few other kids are there already, splashing and yelling. Somebody splashes me and the water is freezing, but in a good way. I let the water soak me from head to raggedy shoes, glad that you can't stutter screams.

"All right, all right, that's enough!" Miz Pacey says, too soon for all of us. We groan and protest, but I think she has the same problem with noise as Aunt Kat, because she threatens to get her broom. She shoos us away like flies and we all take off in different directions.

"Let's go to the playground!" yells Walter, still giddy from the water. I shrug. It's probably a good idea to stay outside. Aunt Kat had mumbled something earlier about wiping down the windowsills, and she usually makes me do that kinda thing as a part of her "summer cleaning."

Most of the neighborhood kids are out here running

around, but my attention goes to the courts, where a girl with long red cornrows is shooting baskets. Thing is, she's not missing.

"I think that's the new kid," Walter says. "Let's say hi!"

Walter takes off before I can protest, and though I really don't wanna follow him, I do. Since I'm going to be a Scepter Leaguer, I might as well practice talking to random strangers. My dad and Frankie Bell would do it all the time with no problem. I take a deep breath and head over before Walter embarrasses us both.

"Hi, my name is Walter, and this is my best friend, Xavier. Welcome to the neighborhood! Do you have any brothers? I'm an only child."

The girl barely looks Walter's way. She bounces the ball, *thump thump*, then shoots—*swish!*

"Hey," she says.

"You're moving into that green house, right?"

"Yeah."

Thump thump, swish!

"We live down that way"—Walter points—"and you'll probably see us a lot, especially Xavier."

Walter says "especially Xavier" in this singsongy voice and I sock him on the shoulder.

"Ow!" He laughs before running away. "Bye, new girl!"

Well, this is awkward. Or at least it would be if this

girl was even paying attention to anything other than her ball. Still, I know I can't just *stand* here; I gotta say something!

"G-g-good thing y-you m-m-moved next to a c-c-court," I say.

She takes another shot. *Swish.*

"It's the *only* good thing about this move."

"R-R-Rosewood t-teams slap in b-b-basketball," I tell her. "If that's wh-where y-you go."

"I heard." She stops dribbling and holds the ball, staring at me. "What's your name?"

"Xavier."

"How many games did they win last season?"

"Huh?"

"The team you said was so good. How many games did they win?"

"Oh." I shrug, cuz I literally have no clue. Cornrow Girl sighs and keeps shooting. I wander away without saying goodbye, *and* without getting her name, which I don't realize until I'm walking home. Hey, at least I talked to her. Frankie Bell would be proud. Aunt Kat, on the other hand, is on level ten when I get inside.

"I tole you, boy! Didn't I tell ya?!" she exclaims, waving an envelope and package at me.

My face is a giant "huh?" Aunt Kat shakes her head and thrusts the envelope toward me. I see my name on the front, but it's already opened. Like, she opened my letter, read it, and didn't even bother putting it back in the envelope. There's no return address, but the postmark says Denver, Colorado.

"Frankie Bell's settin' his sights on you this time," Aunt Kat says.

I look at my name and Aunt Kat's address written in Frankie Bell's curvy handwriting. There's only one sheet of paper, but it feels heavy, like the ink is weighing it down. The letter is folded neat and crisp, almost like it could cut somebody. I hold my breath and read.

Moonie,

If I timed this here letter good enough, it's in your hands right round your twelfth birthday. Now, don't go gettin' excited; I done seen you for each of the other years, and I gotta say, there's nothing too spectacular about you. Yeah, yeah, grab the tissues if you need 'em. This ain't no lovey-dovey letter. Nobody else has the testicular fortitude to tell you this stuff. Listen, when I turned twelve, I started taking piano lessons from Almira Reed. Changed my life in more ways than one. The question is, what are you gonna do at twelve? You ain't no little baby anymore. It's man time, and every man needs a trademark, something to make him stand out from everybody else. Far as I can see, you got nothin', other than the fact that you a wire-mouth, stutterin' boy with jailbird parents. What kinda trademark is that?? So that's why I'm sendin' what I'm sendin'. This is a challenge. An invitation to get your sad self together before I'm on the other side of the dirt. And if you ain't cryin' like a baby right now, I figure you got a chance.

— Frankie Bell

P.S. Take this seriously, Moonie. If that's hard to do, go see Mr. Talbert down the street. Ask him about what happens when you get letters from me.

P.P.S. Tell that old auntie of yours to stop buyin' you raggedy sneakers from the thrift mart. You got feet to show off now.

I read the letter a few times, almost hearing Frankie Bell's scratchy voice saying each word. Dang! He's pretty much calling me a loser and saying no one else is bold enough to tell me. I mean, is being a background dude really that bad? I'm like an extra: the person you need to make up a crowd. I mean, who *really* notices the extras? Nobody. And that's okay.

Right?

I fold the letter and put it back in the envelope. I'm almost scared to see what's in the package.

"Y-y-you opened th-th-that already, too?" I ask. Since I stutter, Aunt Kat usually doesn't think I'm being smart with her. That's one thing she don't get down with. "Be smart in school, not with yo' mouth!" is what she always says.

"Course not," Aunt Kat says, handing the package to me. It's not a box, but one of those bubble envelopes.

"No tellin' what he got in there," Aunt Kat grunts. When it's clear she's waiting for me to open it, that's what I do.

Only thing in the envelope is a pair of navy blue socks with yellow and red polka dots.

"Lord have mercy." Aunt Kat shakes her head and turns up her TV show. "That fool crazy!"

I stare at the socks. *Socks, Frankie Bell?* I turn the package upside down and shake it, but nothing else falls out. I remember Aunt Kat saying our granddaddy used to hide money in random places, so I stick my hand in each sock, hoping to find a five, or at least a dollar. Nothing.

I take everything up to my room and dump it on my bed. I gotta say, the socks do feel super soft. I tie them into a ball and throw them up at the ceiling, seeing how close I can get to the smiley-face dots without actually touching them. When that gets boring, I sit on top of my dresser and watch the neighborhood talk. I can't see down to the playground, but I can hear the ball thumping. I picture Cornrow Girl making every shot.

CHAPTER 3

*"This is a challenge. An invitation to
get your sad self together . . ."*

Aunt Nadine calls today, supposedly to apologize, but Aunt Kat slams the phone down before much of anything is said.

"How so much evil can get into that itty-bitty heart, I do not know," Aunt Kat says, after calling Aunt Nadine a triflin' heifer.

"Dang, Aunt Kat!" I laugh.

"Boy, tell me where the lie is!" Aunt Kat says, raising her eyebrows at me.

I shrug and keep scrubbing at the baseboards. Yeah, Aunt Kat got me today; I'm stuck scrubbing windows, windowsills, and baseboards. Man, these things are dusty as a mug! She lucky I don't have allergies like Walter.

"Why th-they g-gotta be like that?" I ask.

"Boy, that's like asking dirt why it's dirty," Aunt Kat says. "Don't nobody know!"

I drop my rag in an old ice cream bucket filled with vinegar water and squeeze it out.

"Get that one again," Aunt Kat says, pointing at the windowsill I just finished.

I scrub it again, flicking a dead fly into the water.

"I saw that," Aunt Kat says, even though she's not even looking my way. "Dump that outside and get fresh water."

After I get new water, Aunt Kat asks what I'm gonna do with the rest of my day. I probably won't have much of a day left after I finish her chores, but I can't say that. I don't answer right away, cuz the way Aunt Kat asks makes me think about Frankie Bell's toxic letter and his challenge. Like wearing some socks is gonna change things for me.

"Ch-ch-chill in my room, I g-guess," I tell her, starting on the next window. "Or outside."

"With that lil' loud boy?"

The phone rings again before I can say anything, but this time it's someone Aunt Kat actually likes. She laughs and talks all loud about the potholes on Foster Avenue and how her little garden on the side of the house is doing.

"Yeah, me and the nephew gonna be getting at those weeds," she says. My head drops. *Maaaan!*

"You right! I should get his old bones out there, too!" Aunt Kat cackles. I'm guessing she means her "man-friend," Mr. Alvin.

Just when Aunt Kat is talking about making a potato salad for somebody's picnic, there's a ginormous clap of thunder that rattles the house, and she almost drops the phone.

"Sweet Jesus! You hear that, Louise? I gotta let you go, 'fore we both get electrocuted!"

She hangs up the phone with a quickness and turns toward me.

"Come away from that window, boy, before you get struck!" Aunt Kat says.

"By th-th-thunder, Aunt Kat?" I ask, almost laughing, cuz I didn't see any lightning. Aunt Kat always gets super weird when there's a storm. Like now she's humming some kind of church song and closing the curtains on the windows.

"Moonie, just do what I say!" Aunt Kat fusses. "Back-talk me if you wanna; you never know where or when lightning gonna strike. And pour that water out!"

Unlike Frankie Bell, Aunt Kat only calls me Moonie when she's mad, so I get up and do what she says. Thunder shakes the house again, and this time Aunt Kat cusses instead of saying "Sweet Jesus!" I laugh, and she throws her house slipper at me.

"C-c-can I m-make one of those p-p-pizza things?" I ask, handing the slipper to her.

"Boy, sit down somewhere and be still!" Aunt Kat says. "The Lord is doing His work."

Aunt Kat closes her eyes, which is good, cuz she doesn't see me roll mine. I don't know how thunderstorms are God's work, but whatever.

I'm about to ask for a snack or something, but then her eyes pop open.

"Get an apple off the table," she says.

"Can't eat apples," I say, grinning big and pointing at the braces *she* forced me to get. Last time I had an apple, I ended up breaking a few brackets.

"Then get a banana!" Aunt Kat says. "And hush!"

I get the banana and escape upstairs before Aunt Kat makes me take a "the Lord is doing His work" nap. I know that's what she's gonna do. Anytime it rains, she beelines to her easy chair, talkin' about how it's good sleeping weather.

It starts raining hard when I get to my room, so I close my window, climb onto my dresser, and check out what's happening on the block.

Across the street from us, Mrs. Jones is yelling at her kids to come inside, but they're laughing and acting like the hydrant's busted again instead of it being a full-blown rainstorm. A stray dog bounds down the street, probably looking for a porch to climb under. Tree branches move like they're dancing, and the Bryants' basketball hoop is rocking back and forth. I see the Parkers didn't get their sheets off the clothesline in time, and everything's beyond soaked. Across the street and a few houses down, Mr. Talbert's sitting on his porch sipping something from a mug, like the rain don't bother him at all. *Wait . . . Mr. Talbert?*

I grab the package from Frankie Bell off the floor and pull out his letter.

> Take this seriously, Moonie. If that's hard to do, go see Mr. Talbert down the street. Ask him about what happens when you get letters from me.

I watch Mr. Talbert for a good minute, and he doesn't do nothing spectacular, just rocks on his porch sipping whatever it is he's sipping. When a huge thunderclap sounds a few minutes later, I jump and almost fall off the dresser. But Mr. Talbert doesn't even flinch at all. I guess I shouldn't be shocked because Mr. Talbert's kind of a different dude. He's always at our bus stop in the mornings, handing out peppermints and saying corny motivational school stuff, and his hands and clothes always look dusty, like he hangs out in an old, dusty attic. None of the adults tell us to stay away from him, though. Why in the world would Frankie Bell be sending *him* letters?

I leave the window and lay out on my bed with my Switch. I play until my eyes get heavy. Maybe rainstorms *are* good sleeping weather. But even as I'm falling asleep, I can't stop thinking about the socks and Frankie Bell's challenge. Aunt Kat was right; Frankie Bell's mind games are starting to get to me!

CHAPTER 4

*"I DARE you to see what happens
when you do."*

Okay, here's the deal. I, Xavier "Moonie" Moon, am *not* crazy. But I'll tell you who is . . . Frankie Bell! It's three days before school starts, and he sent me *another* package!

Moonie,

I'll bet my left kidney you ain't wore the socks yet. You probably balled 'em up and threw 'em on the floor. Don't just stand there like a pillar of salt, Moonie; get on with it! Whatcha waitin' for, chest hair to appear? I'ma say it again, if you don't get yourself together this year, it might never happen, and I might not ever see it. Gotta have confidence, no matter what! It don't matter how dumb or ugly or short somebody is; doors will open left and right when you

got CONFIDENCE, or as y'all youngbloods say, swag.
Yeah, I know that word. I got a guy with me right
now, ugly as the devil's bottom, but once he starts
smiling and talking to the ladies, you would swear
he's Denzel Washington, and they apparently think
so, too! School's out, Moonie, but I'm giving you some
homework. 1. Walk with your head up and shoulders
straight. 2. Pretend you're Denzel, or whoever else
them little girls whoop and holler over nowadays.
3. Wear the socks; I DARE you to see what happens
when you do.
                              —Frankie Bell

P.S. Tell that aunt of yours to quit worryin' 'bout where
I'm at. She needs to worry about your hair. Tell her to
stop taking you to that half-blind fool on Worthington
Avenue. Tell her to take you to Percy, over on McCary.
He owes me a favor, and you owe yourself a haircut
that don't look like Halloween.

I fold up Frankie Bell's letter and stare at the floor,
where the socks are balled up, half under my bed. The
postmark on this envelope says Austin, Texas, and when
I empty out the bubble envelope, a new pair of socks
tumbles out. Black with neon green stripes.

Okay, I'm officially done. I drop the socks like they're

infested. I look at my clothes and then at the socks, and I'm low-key freaking out. Before this package got here, I had grabbed a pair of black jean shorts from the floor and a green polo shirt from my clean-clothes basket. It's almost like I was meant to wear the black-and-green socks today. No way Frankie Bell would know that . . . right? And why's he daring me to wear them? What's supposed to happen?

"Get dressed, Moonie!" Aunt Kat bangs on my door and I jump like I'm doing something wrong. "We goin' to your school and to US Thrift!"

I groan, but not loud enough for her to hear. Aunt Kat refuses to call the store by its right name, *U.S. Thrift*. She walks around saying "US Thrift" instead.

"Okay!" I call to Aunt Kat.

There's a rectangular mirror on the back of my door, and after I pull the socks on, I walk over and check myself out.

Frankie Bell's right about my haircut. Shannon says I have nice hair and shouldn't cut it, but I think it's too thick and curly. I'd look much better with a fresh cut. Gotta make sure that happens before school starts.

The socks don't look bad. They're definitely not what other dudes wear. I hold my head up and straighten my shoulders like Frankie Bell said.

"Yo, w-w-wassup?" I say to my reflection. I pretend I'm talking to the fine girls at school. "Y-you look n-n-nice t-today."

"Moonie! Ain't gonna call you again!" Aunt Kat says.

I do one last mirror check and head downstairs.

Aunt Kat takes one look at me when I come into the kitchen and shakes her head when she sees the socks.

"Now, what's that supposed to be?" she asks. I shrug. I'm trying not to mention anything about the second package from Frankie Bell cuz I can tell it'll send her into a mood.

"That ol' fool," she says under her breath before handing me a plate of biscuits, cheese grits, hash browns, eggs, and bacon.

Uh-oh.

Whenever Aunt Kat makes a breakfast like this, it means we gonna be out for a while. She don't like fast food, so she tries to stuff me before we leave.

I sit at the table and spread strawberry jelly all over my biscuits.

"So he's still sending you socks?"

My mouth is full of grits, so I nod.

Aunt Kat shakes her head again.

"W-why you th-th-think he d-does that?"

"How'm I ta know?" Aunt Kat asks. "That man has

a mind of his own! Always done peculiar stuff like that since he was knee-high to a grasshopper. Used to chew each bite of cornflakes exactly ten times, and button his shirts from the bottom up. And he knew it irritated the stuffing out of us, too! Always had this look on his face like he knew we were three skips and a hop from pulling our hair out on account of him!"

"He ever s-s-send you stuff?" I ask.

"Not no undergarments; that's for sure!" Aunt Kat says. "Mostly letters or postcards."

Aunt Kat stabs a piece of egg and points the fork at me. "There was this one time he went on the road, though, and this fool sent me dirt from every city he played in. Dirt! In every envelope! I tell you, I poured each envelope of dirt onto his pillow, so when he got home, he had a nice pile to remind him of his travels. Had the nerve to call himself 'offended' that I didn't appreciate his gift."

Aunt Kat calls Frankie Bell a name under her breath, and I don't ask any more questions. She's known her brother for, like, a hundred years, so I guess she's had much more time than me to be annoyed by him. I know she loves him. She goes down to the basement, which is his space, when she thinks we don't see her. Guess it's cuz he's the only sibling she got left. I'm thinking maybe Shannon would do the same thing with me, and I wonder if we'll act like Aunt Kat and Frankie Bell when we're old.

"Get s'more of this," Aunt Kat says, dumping a mound of hash browns on my plate before I can stop her.

"Aunt K-K-Kat, I'm g-good," I tell her.

"Yeah, you betta stay good," she tells me, "cuz you know I ain't stoppin' at no Mike Donald's or anywhere else!"

I force the food down and follow Aunt Kat to the car. Riding with her is always interesting, cuz she talks about how *other* people drive, when she be doing reckless stuff, too!

We make it to my school in one piece, with Aunt Kat only blowing her horn at one person. When I open my door and climb out the car, I see something green fluttering by my foot. *Is that what I think it is?* I reach down fast, and yup, it's a five-dollar bill! I stuff it in my pocket and follow Aunt Kat to the main office with a smile on my face.

"Well, hi, Xavier! How's the summer going?" Mrs. Miller asks when we walk in. I like how she always knows our names.

"Great," I say, showing all my braces. Something about finding money makes everything better.

"And what can I do for you all?"

"I mainly need to make sure he got speech services this school year," Aunt Kat says.

"Yes, ma'am, I do see that in his record. Let me print

a copy of his schedule." Mrs. Miller walks to the printer, and Aunt Kat just keeps going. She tells Mrs. Miller that I would stumble over words sometimes when I was little but things seem to have gotten worse lately.

"Y'all are supposed to be helpin' him! Sometimes he barely talks cuz he afraid he's 'bout to do it! Now, I can't have a no-talkin' boy up in my house, you hear what I'm sayin'?"

"Maaaan," I mumble. I love Aunt Kat, but I wish my mom was here instead. Or my dad. That's probably what would really help me. Cuz if I started stuttering bad when they left, I'm guessing I'll stop when they come home.

"Boy, hush! I'm tryin' to help you get right!" she tells me. "Now, who was your speech lady last year?"

"M-M-Ms. Nixon."

"Well, I can tell you we have Mr. Garadagio joining our team this year," Mrs. Miller says.

"Gara-who?" Aunt Kat interrupts, her voice going up, like, three octaves on the "who?"

"Mr. G usually works much better."

Aunt Kat and I whirl around and see a guy standing at the office door. He's wearing khaki shorts, a yellow-striped polo shirt, and brown loafers with no socks. Also, he's got a sunshine tattoo on his arm, and his hair is doing the same spiky thing as that dude on the Food Network show that Shannon loves. He holds out his hand to Aunt Kat, who looks at it like he just pulled it from the toilet. Then she shakes it.

"And who are you?" she asks.

"Anthony Garadagio," he says. "Better known as Mr. G. And may I ask your name?"

"You may," Aunt Kat says. "I'm Katherine Bell, better known as Kat. *Aunt* Kat to this boy."

"Very pleased to meet you." Mr. G turns to me. "And what's your name?"

"Xavier."

"Awesome name," Mr. G says, holding out his fist for me to dap. "I named a fish Xavier once."

"So, Mr. Anthony," Aunt Kat begins.

"Mr. G," Mr. G corrects her.

"Mr. *Anthony*," Aunt Kat continues, "I ain't callin' no teacher by no letter."

"Mr. Anthony will be fine, ma'am," Mr. G says with a smile. He's catching on fast, at least. "And I'm looking forward to working with Xavier this year."

"Hmmph. Well, nice to meet ya." Aunt Kat thanks Mrs. Miller and we head out.

"Oh, by the way, I'm lovin' the socks, Xavier." Mrs. Miller gives me a thumbs-up and winks.

In the hallway outside the office, something on the

bulletin board catches my eye. A green-and-gold flyer with big, bold writing that stops me in my tracks.

If you're ready for the next level right now, Scepter League might be for you!

The flyer has a picture of a green blazer with the Scepter League logo on the front and all the requirements to get in. The interest meeting is in two weeks, at the rec center on Union. The information is nothing new to me—almost got it memorized. But now I'm actually seeing myself in that blazer. I'll wear it on the day Dad gets out. Yeah. That'll blow his mind!

"Ah Lawd, you starin' at that poster like it's a girlie magazine." Aunt Kat shakes her head.

"Wh-what?" I pull my eyes from the flyer and look at the huge smirk on Aunt Kat's face.

"Naw, you ain't gotta stutter through an explanation," she says. "It all makes perfect sense now, the socks, the letters; you 'bout to be a Frankie Bell mini-me!"

Aunt Kat shakes her head and keeps walking toward the door, yelling at me to stop drooling and come on. On the drive, she doesn't say anything else about the Scepter League, but I wonder if she's right. Is Frankie Bell trying to turn me into a mini-him?

When we finally get to U.S. Thrift, Aunt Kat makes a wild turn into the parking lot and almost takes out some guy on one of those explore-the-city bikes. Jeez! She's out the car before me, anxious to get inside cuz it's a "red tag sale," whatever that means.

"C'mon now, you gotta keep up with me," Aunt Kat says. "We gonna come outta here with all your school clothes; you watch and see!"

If clothes shopping was a competitive sport, Aunt Kat would have a gold medal. She's grabbing jeans and shirts and jackets off the rack at lightning speed, and each time she finds something with a red tag, she says, "Half off, baby!"

While Aunt Kat goes wild with the clothes, I wander over to the shoe section. Usually the shoes here are either for little kids or for people Frankie Bell's age. Today must be my lucky day, though, because right in front of my face is a pair of green-and-black Jordans. I pick them up to check out the size, and the number 8 looks back at me. Even better, there's a red tag attached!

"Half off, baby!" I say, grinning as I go find Aunt Kat.

"C-can I get these, Aunt Kat?" I hold 'em up so the tag's facing her. Aunt Kat squints at the shoes, then takes them from me and studies them.

"These them expensive shoes?" she asks.

"Yeah, b-b-but look." I point to the tag and her face changes a little.

"Good price," she says, putting them into the over-flowing cart. *Yes!* "Now you go try these things on. Try on everything, y'hear? They don't let you return nothing after you buy it."

I'm not even mad that I have to try on a hundred pairs of pants and shirts while Aunt Kat shops for stuff for her. Mostly everything fits, and there are only a few things I wouldn't be caught dead wearing. Aunt Kat even finds some old-lady swag, and we make our way to the checkout feelin' pretty good.

"Oh, these are a great buy," the cashier says when she rings up the shoes. She frowns a little and pauses. "I wonder if we tagged them wrong. We don't usually red-tag new shoes."

"Well, ya did today!" Aunt Kat says, taking the shoes from the lady's hand and putting them in one of the bags. She gives the lady a look like, "You bet' not check with a manager!" The lady moves on to ringing up the rest of our stuff.

"Those shoes were one lucky deal," she says again after Aunt Kat pays for everything. "You got a cool pair of shoes to match your super-cool socks."

Oh snap!

I glance down. I forgot about the socks, but it's the second time somebody's mentioned them. And since I put them on today, all kinds of lucky stuff has been happening. First the money, and now I got new Jays that are the same color as the socks? For a split second, I wonder if maybe Frankie Bell really *is* magic. If he is, I'm definitely gonna accept his challenge.

When I get into the Scepter League, he's gonna find out I got the magic, too.

CHAPTER 5

*"Gotta have confidence,
no matter what!"*

"Hey, there's the new girl!" Walter says, before screaming, "HEEEEEY, NEW GIRL!!" and waving his arm off. We're shooting hoops on one end of the basketball court, and Cornrow Girl is walking our way, basketball under her arm. She gives us a nod and goes right to what she does best: making shots.

"She's really good, right?" Walter says. He throws a wild pass my way, and since I'm staring at Cornrow Girl, it almost hits me in the head.

"C'mon, W-Walter!"

"Sorry, sorry!" he says. "We should go play with her."

"Nah," I say. Me and sports are a disaster together, which is a shame cuz Shannon runs track and plays volleyball, and both my parents played basketball in high school. Ma is always telling the story of how she beat my dad in one-on-one and he loved her ever since. Guess all those good genes skipped me.

The good stuff skipped Walter, too, because his next shot hits the rim and ricochets to the other side of the court. I jog over to grab the ball, and Cornrow Girl actually stops shooting long enough to notice me!

"So what's with the socks?" she asks.

I look at the socks like I'm seeing them for the first time and shrug like it's no big deal. Baby blue with lightning bolts. Frankie Bell said people would either admire my socks or hate on them, but I gotta act like it doesn't matter to me either way.

"It's m-m-my thing," I say. That would've come out better without the stutter, but oh well.

"Cool," she says. She looks at my socks again and I feel like I should say something else, but then I hear the song "Pop! Goes the Weasel" in the distance and getting closer. Ice cream truck.

Kids start rushing toward it, and of course, Walter's one of them.

"Oooohhh! I want ice cream!" Walter squeals. He digs his hands in his pockets and comes up empty. "Xavier, you got money?"

I touch my pocket, where I know I got six dollar

bills folded neatly. Frankie Bell came in clutch with his third letter; he sent me ten bucks with these lightning bolt socks. He said that swag don't mix with empty pockets. I already spent four on a wallet, cuz that's what Frankie Bell said I should buy first. I hate to spend the rest of it, but Cornrow Girl *is* staring at the ice cream truck pretty hard. By the time Walter runs home to beg his mom for money, like he's about to do, the truck will be gone.

I stand up.

"Y'all w-w-w-w-want ice cream?" I ask.

"Yeah!" Walter jumps up and down. "Buy some for the new girl, too!"

"I g-g-got y'all," I say, hoping my cash is enough.

The line is mad long, and by the time we get to the front, the guy is out of Firecracker Popsicles, which Walter wants, *and* strawberry Good Humor bars, which is what Cornrow Girl asks for.

"Aww man!" Walter pouts.

"Tell you what, tell you what," the guy says, a gold tooth glinting from his mouth. "Ice cream sandwiches on the house, aight? Cuz lil' man's socks are fiyah!"

I kinda wanted a Snickers ice cream bar, but free is free. The ice cream guy hands me the sandwiches, and when I take them, he makes a fist for me to dap.

"Right on, lil' man," he says with a wink.

Some kids who got their ice cream before us go, "That ain't fair!" when they see we got ours for free.

"Ay, come and see me when you got sock game like that kid," I hear the ice cream guy tell them.

Whoa.

Sock game.

First I found the money at my school. Then the Jordans were on sale and Aunt Kat actually got them. Now I'm getting free ice cream? Yo, this sock thing is magic! Frankie Bell put a swag-spell on them or something. I feel like a kid in some lame Disney Channel movie, and I almost wish Frankie Bell was here so I could tell him I took him up on his dare and I believe now.

I open my ice cream sandwich, take a huge bite, and check out the socks again. When I look up, Cornrow Girl's eyes are on them, too. Then her eyes are on mine.

"So that's why you wear those socks?" she asks, a curious look on her face. "They're, like, lucky or something?"

"M-maybe," I say. And because I'm pretty sure Frankie Bell would do this, I just grin and walk away like it's no biggie.

I still got the grin on my face when I walk home, and I don't notice Mr. Talbert sitting on his porch at first.

"Way you grinnin', you musta won a million bucks!"

he calls when I'm about to pass his house. Lucky for me, I don't jump too much.

"H-hey, Mr. T-T-Talbert," I say.

"How you doing there, Xavier Moon?"

"I'm g-g-good," I say.

"How Frankie Bell doin'?" Mr. Talbert asks, which reminds me that I'm supposed to be talking to him. I stop walking and tell him Frankie Bell is on the road again. Mr. Talbert smiles.

"Well, that don't surprise me none! Frankie always stayed on the move," he says.

"H-h-how you kn-know him?" I ask, walking a little closer to Mr. Talbert's porch.

"Frankie Bell? Been knowin' him since he moved up from Alabama; been neighbors on this street most of our lives."

"He ever, l-like, s-send you letters?" I ask, feeling dumb as soon as the words come out my mouth. But Mr. Talbert just chuckles.

"Yes, he did. He surely did. Wasn't something I ever expected, but I tell you what: them letters saved my life."

Mr. Talbert stares off down the block and doesn't say anything else. I stand there awkwardly waiting for him to say *how* the letters saved his life, but it's almost like he forgot I'm here.

"Well, b-bye, Mr. T-Talbert," I say, giving a wave.

"All right, son, you take care now," Mr. Talbert says.

I head down the block to Aunt Kat's house, wondering what Frankie Bell wrote to Mr. Talbert. Whatever it was, if it worked for Mr. Talbert's life, it's gotta work for mine.

CHAPTER 6

*"I don't need no speech.
A man does less talkin', more doin',
you understand me?"*

Saturdays mean a phone call with Ma, and today it comes right after breakfast.

Ma's voice is like the honey I pour over one of Aunt Kat's fluffy biscuits. Thick and sweet, kinda like Beyoncé's. When I tell her about Frankie Bell sending me socks, she busts out laughing.

"I'm not even surprised," she says. "When I was little, he went on the road one time and brought me spoons from every restaurant he ate at! Said it was cuz I'm always stirring things up."

We talk about Frankie Bell for a while, and Ma still has a smile in her voice when we have to hang up.

"Hey, Shannon, y-y-you think I can write Frankie Bell b-b-back?"

Aunt Kat went to the casino, so I'm getting some undisturbed action out of my Nintendo Switch, and Shannon's bingeing on Netflix.

"I don't know," Shannon says with a yawn. "He's usually city to city, so where would you send a letter to? Just text him or something."

She's right, of course. But if Frankie Bell's anything like Aunt Kat, he won't know how to text. I really wanna ask him more about the socks and tell him that whatever he did to them is working.

"He ever s-s-s-send you weird stuff?" I ask, thinking about Ma and the spoons.

"He sent me a doll once," Shannon says. "It was only weird cuz I was, like, thirteen and didn't play with dolls anymore. I still have her, though."

"Is it, like, lucky?" I ask.

"It's a *doll*, Xav," Shannon says, like, *duh!*

Maybe it's dumb to think the socks have powers. I'm wearing orange-and-red-striped socks, and so far nothing special's happening.

Then Shannon's phone buzzes and she groans when she looks at it.

"Hello?"

Shannon closes her eyes as she listens to whoever's on the other end.

"Yeah, okay. I can be there in thirty."

When she hangs up, she sighs all extra.

"Gotta cover for Chrissy, cuz she's 'sick,'" she says, throwing up air quotes. Shannon works at a Greens 'n Things, this healthy restaurant a few blocks away. She's the youngest person there, but you wouldn't be able to tell. She takes that job real serious, says it's a stepping stone to bigger and better.

"J-J-Ju gonna take you?" I ask. I'm hoping I can get some pointers from him about the interest meeting next Saturday.

"Nah, he has a Scepter League meeting today." Shannon nudges me and grins. Ever since she found out I'm trying to join the League, she's been making little comments about me getting in.

"Man, quit!" I say, pulling away from her. She laughs and runs upstairs to change. I can't hide my grin, though. I'm only a week away from the interest meeting, and then everything changes. I start practicing the Scepter League Creed out loud, deep breaths, sitting up straight and holding my head up high. I got this.

"Make sure you lock the door. And don't go outside," Shannon tells me as she heads out.

"I *know,*" I say. Jeez, she acts like I'm still six sometimes. Aunt Kat says Shannon can't help it; ever since I was born she's acted like a second mom. She really went bananas with it when Ma got in trouble.

I heat up three hot dogs and demolish them while watching Netflix. I get up and stuff one of Aunt Kat's coffee mugs with ice cream, but then the phone rings and I almost drop the mug to answer it.

"Hello?"

"Moonie? That you?"

Frankie Bell's scratchy voice and a whole lotta background noise fills the line.

"Y-y-yeah," I say. "H-hi, Frankie B-Bell."

"Oh yeah, that's you all right," Frankie Bell chuckles. "How you doin', nephew?"

"G-good," I say. "Y-you?"

"I'm livin' and breathin', and this fox thinks I'm leavin'!" Frankie Bell laughs. I hear him say something that sounds like "Just a second, baby" to someone, and I fight to keep from gagging. After a few moments of muffled talking, Frankie Bell's voice is clear again.

"Moonie, you been doin' what you supposed to be doin'?"

He must mean the socks.

"Y-yeah, I b-been wearing them every day, and I'm g-g-gonna—"

"Naw, naw," Frankie Bell interrupts right before I tell

him about the Scepter League. "I don't need no speech. A man does less talkin', more doin', you understand me? 'Long as you doin', I don't need to hear nothin' more."

Ummm, okay. I have no idea what to say, so I keep quiet while Frankie Bell yells that someone named Leroy is moving like molasses going uphill.

"Where's your aunt Kat?" he asks me after he finishes cussing the Leroy guy out.

"At the c-c-casino," I tell him.

"Casino? Yeah, she would be there when I call," Frankie Bell says with a grumble. "Well, look here, you just tell her I put some duckets in the bank; she'll know what to do with that."

Duckets? What in the world is that?

"O-kay, I'll t-tell her," I say. "Where are you?"

"I'm everywhere I need to be," Frankie Bell says.

After a few seconds of me not knowing what to say (again), Frankie Bell says he has to go, and not in normal words.

"Horn player soundin' like he poured gravy down the mouthpiece," Frankie Bell grunts. "See ya up the mountain, Moonie."

He's gone before I can say goodbye.

I hang up the phone and stare at my mug of melting ice cream. Aunt Kat don't like us wasting nothin', so I eat spoonful after spoonful till it's gone. I try to keep watching my Netflix show, but my mind keeps drifting to my weird uncle. I take my dishes to the sink, check outside for Aunt Kat's car, and quietly open the basement door.

I only been down here once since me and Shannon moved in, and that was only because Frankie Bell needed me to help him carry some boxes. It's an unspoken rule that none of us can be in his space. Frankie Bell mostly uses the outside entrance, so we don't always know whether he's home or not. I think he likes it that way.

Twelve steps to get to the bottom, and then I'm in Frankie Bell's world. There's a cot against the wall that's made up super neat like it's a hotel bed or something. Frankie Bell's piano is across from his cot, and even though it's brown and shiny, I can tell it's really old. I touch the keys lightly, then wander over to another door, which opens to a tiny bathroom with just a toilet, sink, and the smallest shower I've ever seen. It smells like Frankie Bell's cologne and aftershave.

I pick up one of Frankie Bell's hats and put it on my head, slightly tilted, the way he always wears it. I check myself out in the tall mirror that's beside his dresser.

"Hey now," I say, making my voice low and sing-y like his. "How y'all doin'? What's y'all's favorite jam?"

I saunter over to the piano and sit down.

"See how you like this one." I pretend I'm Frankie Bell, curling my fingers on the keys and shaking my head like I'm really feeling it. I'm in the middle of applauding myself when I hear Aunt Kat's car roar into the driveway. I jump up, snatch Frankie Bell's hat off my head, and race upstairs. I'm breathing heavy on the couch, flipping through an Obama magazine when Aunt Kat shuffles in.

"Hey, Aunt K-Kat," I say.

"Hey, baby," she says. "What you been getting into?"

"Umm, n-nothing," I tell her. *Did I turn off the light in the basement?* "Shannon h-h-had to work."

"Mmm-hmm, she sent me one of them text message thingies," Aunt Kat says. "You eat already?"

"Not really."

"Well, I feel like a nice salad, whatchoo think?" Aunt Kat asks. It's kind of our inside joke, cuz neither one of us likes salad, but Shannon always makes us eat one when she cooks.

"Nah, Aunt Kat," I say with a grin.

"No salad?" Aunt Kat pretends to be shocked. "I guess we'll just have to have meatloaf and mashed potatoes, then. Come on and help me peel these thangs."

I stop fake-reading the magazine and join Aunt Kat in the kitchen. For some reason, I love peeling potatoes. I take the skin off in long, easy glides until the potato is perfectly white, like the keys on Frankie Bell's piano.

"Wh-wh-what's your thing, Aunt K-Kat?" I ask.

"My *thing?*" Aunt Kat's eyebrows bunch together.

"Y-yeah. Frankie B-Bell's is p-piano, m-m-my dad's is c-cars, Sh-Shannon's is c-cooking. Wh-what's yours?"

"Hmmph." Aunt Kat thinks for a minute. "I suppose it would be my garden. Always did keep a garden, you know. Flowers, vegetables, don't matter to me; I just love seein' thangs grow. Got that from my daddy."

As Aunt Kat goes on about different things she's grown, I think about Frankie Bell's first letter. I think he's right: everybody needs a trademark to set them apart. So when am I gonna find mine?

CHAPTER 7

*"Walk with your head up and
shoulders straight."*

"Hey, Xavier!"

Walter's face is the first thing I see when I open the front door, and he scares the mess outta me. He giggles at the cuss word that slips out my mouth.

"Ooooh!" he says with a laugh.

"Shut up," I say. "Wh-wh-wh-what you d-doin' here?"

First day of school and it *would* be Walter to be up early when he don't have to be. I mean, his bus comes a whole hour after mine!

"Gonna hang out with Mr. Talbert," Walter says. "Think he's gonna be here this year?"

"I guess," I say, slinging my bookbag over my shoulder and locking the front door.

"C'mon, let's go see!"

Walter is literally bouncing up and down, which is

totally unnecessary for 6:52 in the morning. Of course, he's talking nonstop.

"I had waffles for breakfast," he says. "Strawberry jam on top. I tried to get some of Mom's coffee, but she went like this to my hand." Walter smacks his hand and laughs. "What did you eat?"

"Oatmeal."

Aunt Kat don't use those flavored packets of oatmeal like the rest of the world. Nah, her oatmeal is thick as mud. She says it'll stick to my ribs, which sounds physically impossible, until you taste her oatmeal. The good thing is she uses a lot of brown sugar and sometimes she throws on blueberries and granola. Bad thing is, I usually gotta take a dump after a bowl.

"Oatmeal's good, I guess," Walter says, but his face is scrunched up like he doesn't really mean it. "I like grits, with honey on top."

"You're w-w-weird, Walter," I say, shaking my head. He doesn't even miss a beat, just hops off my steps and starts moving. He keeps running in front of me, then slowing down so I can catch up.

"Look, there he is!" Walter says, pointing up ahead.

I slow down a bit, let Walter zoom off while I study Mr. Talbert. He has on classic old-man clothes: corduroy-looking pants, short-sleeve button-up shirt with a glasses case in the front pocket, and those old-people shoes with Velcro. His hair reminds me of a cloud, all white and fluffy. When I get closer, I see he's got a gold chain hanging around his neck, kinda like the one Frankie Bell wears. I wonder what their connection is anyway. I almost walk right up to him to find out, but then I decide there's too many kids around to ask.

Walter's super excited to see Mr. Talbert. I don't know why this kid likes hangin' with people who are older than him. But Walter ain't the only one; other kids crowd around Mr. Talbert like he's Santa or something.

The bus makes one stop on Larmity, and it's in front of Mr. Talbert's house. For the two years I've lived with Aunt Kat, he's always outside early in the morning, passing out peppermints to the kids waiting for the bus. Aunt Kat says he's been doing it since before Jesus turned water to wine.

"Walt-man!" Mr. Talbert says as Walter bum-rushes him with a hug. His voice is scratchy, and kinda country, but it sounds, I don't know, familiar. Like Frankie Bell's a little. "How ya doin', young man?"

"Good!" Walter's bouncing up and down. *Dang, chill, dude!* Absolutely no swag!

"Xavier Moon," Mr. Talbert says, the way he always does. Man, just because I'm Frankie Bell's great-nephew don't mean I gotta be first and last name like him. "First day of school; how you feelin'?"

"Good."

"Just 'good'?" Mr. Talbert says. He hands me a peppermint. "You can do better than that! 'Specially with them snazzy socks!"

Snazzy? That makes me wanna take these socks off and burn 'em! They're white with different-colored crayons all over them, and they go pretty good with the blue Converse I've had forever and the jean shorts we got at U.S. Thrift. Frankie Bell said I might as well be school-themed on the first day. The postmark on his last package said Boston, Massachusetts, so I guess he was around all those Ivy Leagues when he sent these.

Frankie Bell's latest letter also said I only get one shot to make a good impression and that all kinds of eyes will be on me. Yeah, not creepy at all. He was trying to be all deep, like, who do you want to be on Day 1, and who do you want to be on Day 180?

It's really pretty simple. I'm gonna be Upgraded Xavier from Day 1. I know I'm not this cool musician dude who everyone (including girls) loves and worships. But at least I'll be known for having sock swag.

Or not.

"Snazzy socks" is definitely not the look I'm going for. Mr. Talbert's over here killing my first-day-of-school vibe!

The bus rumbles to a stop in front of us, and some

kids run up the steps like it's the ice cream truck. Others trudge forward with a sigh, like the whole world just got dumped in their bookbags. I'm more in the middle— a tiny bit nervous, but also ready to beast-mode this first day. I walk up the steps like I own the bus.

"Bye, Xavier!" Walter yells, waving his bony arm off. I hear a few people snicker, so I don't turn around to wave back. I feel kinda bad, but hey, the kid's gotta learn to make friends his own age.

"Carpe diem!" Mr. Talbert calls to all of us, raising a fist.

I shake my head. He says that every day, all excited, too. Walter better watch out; if he keeps hanging around Mr. Talbert, he might turn into the next weird old guy who watches kids go to school.

I walk to the middle of the bus, drop my bag on the seat, and sit down. Kids are talking, laughing, joking— all the normal stuff—and as usual, I'm quiet. After a few more stops, the bus crowds up. When we pull onto McIntire, a group of, like, fifteen kids piles on, mostly girls. I'm expecting all of them to head to the back, where a lot of guys are. But a few stop in the middle, and one of them actually Looks. Right. At. Me.

"Can I sit with you?" she asks.

"Y-yeah," I say quickly, grabbing my bookbag and

scooting to the window. She plops down beside me, and I'm like, *Yo! Maybe* this *is why Mr. Talbert be handing out mints!*

Say something, say something, say something! I tell myself. I picture Frankie Bell sitting here with a cute girl and wonder what he would say. Probably some stuff I'd get in trouble for repeating.

"OMG, your socks are so cool!" the girl says, staring at my feet. Her friends are sitting across from her, so of course she puts my socks on blast.

"Shyanne! Look at his socks!"

Shyanne leans forward and I recognize her from last year. She's in seventh grade like me.

"'S-sup, Shyanne," I say with a nod.

"Hey, Xavier," she says. "Crayons, though?"

"I think they're fiyah." Her friend shrugs, pulling out her cell phone. "Hold out your foot. Xavier, right?"

She wanna take a pic of my socks? Is she serious right now? Turns out she is. Man, I am glad I listened to Aunt Kat when she yelled at me about putting on lotion!

Shyanne's friend—or wait, I think it's her cousin—snaps a few pics and asks if I mind her posting them.

"This gonna go on my first-day-of-school story," she says.

"You do too much, Renee," Shyanne says.

"N-nah, it's c-c-cool," I say. I'm about to ask her what her IG name is, but then she turns in her seat and talks nonstop with Shyanne and them the rest of the way. No worries; I got her name, so I don't have to say nothing else. Plus, she gonna remember me for these socks.

As soon as I get into the school lobby, I run into my boys. Actually, I hear them before I see them.

"Yo, Xavier! Bro, what are you, a whole crayon box?"

Latrell checks out my socks with a laugh and holds his fist out for dap.

"I'm j-j-just s-sayin', this c-c-crayon b-box s-sat n-next to her the whole b-b-bus ride," I say, nodding to where the girl is walking.

"Whatever, bro," Adam laughs. "She's, like, in eighth grade."

I just shrug and grin.

"Okay, I see you," Latrell says. He takes out a brush and runs it over his head. "Y'all going to the lunchroom?"

I nod, even though my stomach is stuffed with oatmeal.

"Yo, that's 'bout to be me." Latrell elbows me as we sit down. I turn around and immediately see what he's talking about.

Scepter Leaguers.

They always rock their gear on the first day of school, and there are some guys wearing green and gold a few tables away. Eighth graders who got in last year. You gotta be in seventh grade to even do the interest meeting and application.

Adam sucks his teeth as me and Latrell watch the Leaguers while trying not to *look* like we're watching them.

"Man, I ain't trying to wear church clothes to school all the time and recite stupid stuff." Adam makes his voice all high and goes, "*'I am a man who lights the way for others.'*"

"Yeah, whatever," Latrell laughs, and slurps down his milk carton. "That's why you got the creed memorized!"

"I'ma do football," Adam says. "Whatchoo gonna do, Xavier? Chess or something?"

They both bust up laughing.

"N-nah, bro," I say. "I'm 'b-bout to b-be in the League, t-t-too."

Adam's eyes bug out his head like this the craziest thing that could ever happen. Dang. Latrell's do, too, but he's more excited than doubtful.

"Yo, for real? You comin' to the meeting on Saturday?"

I nod and Latrell gives me dap.

"That's what I'm talkin' about, bro! Your dad was one, too, right?"

"Yeah, and m-m-my uncle," I say.

"My pops is mad excited about it," Latrell says.

"S-s-same," I say, even though I haven't mentioned it to Dad at all. I'm thinking it can be a surprise for when he gets out. Yeah. He'll come home and see we have matching jackets.

Adam keeps hating on me and Latrell, but we tune him out. When the bell rings, we compare schedules. We lucked out and have two classes together, Innovation Lab and Art.

Innovation Lab sounds kinda cool, like maybe we'll build robots or something. The classroom is set up with lab tables, so I'm sure we'll do experiments. Latrell heads to a table in the back and me and Adam follow him.

Latrell slumps in his chair, stretches his legs, and groans extra loud.

"Bro, I haaaaate school!"

"Yo, shut up!" Adam says, watching our teacher walk into the room. Latrell's notorious for getting people in trouble. This one time, he made a joke about Ms. Howard's ashy ankles and I busted out laughing in the middle of a test. Ms. Howard made me move my desk up close by her and I couldn't concentrate cuz I kept looking at her feet. No lie, they *were* pretty ashy.

"So?" Latrell says, making a face like he don't care about the teacher. "That dude probably hates school, too!"

Our teacher's name is Mr. Kirk, and when he introduces himself, Latrell immediately asks, "Like Captain

Kirk?" Some kids laugh, which is pretty much like giving Latrell money.

Mr. Kirk smiles a little.

"No, like Mr. Kirk," he says. "You can write it on the board for me if you think you'll forget."

"Oooh," somebody says, and Latrell sucks his teeth. But he keeps quiet while Mr. Kirk goes on and on with first-day rules and stuff. I'm just getting a good yawn in when an announcement comes over the intercom.

"Xavier Moon is needed in the main office. Xavier Moon, please come to the main office."

"Yo, you in trouble already?" Adam asks. Latrell shakes his head like he's *sooo* disappointed. I don't get up right away cuz I'm wondering what in the world I could've possibly done in, like, thirty minutes.

I'm also thinking about the last time I got called down to the office. Fourth grade. Mrs. Patterson had us doing silent reading, so the voice on the scratchy intercom sounded super loud. Everybody was jealous that I got to leave class. Shannon was pacing in the office when I got there, and she had this fierce look on her face. The first thing she told me to do was tie my shoe. She didn't say anything else until we got home and I found out Ma and Dad weren't there.

"Xavier?" Mr. Kirk is looking at me. "They're calling you to the office."

I slowly get to my feet and leave the class. As I walk down the hall, I think about what it could be. Shannon, with more bad news. Maybe something happened to Aunt Kat. She *is* pretty old. Or maybe I gotta see Mr. G about my stuttering.

I stop before I get to the office and stare at the Scepter League poster again.

the next level right now

The next level right now.

I take a deep breath and tell myself that no matter who's on the other side of this door, I'm not gonna be the same Xavier as before.

I open the office door, and . . . no Shannon. I guess that's good. Actually, there's no one else in here except the secretary. Mrs. Miller looks up when she sees me and smiles.

"Hi, Xavier!" she says.

"Hey," I tell her. "Th-they called me d-d-down."

"Yes, yes, we did." Mrs. Miller has a slight frown on her face that makes me nervous as she looks at her computer. "If you have a seat right there, Mrs. Tynes will be with you in a second."

I sit down in a chair that squeaks and glance down

the short hall to Mrs. Tynes's office. She's the guidance counselor, so I'm trying to figure out how I could be in trouble with her when some kid comes out her office. He's holding a paper in his hand and he doesn't look happy. Great. Mrs. Tynes isn't too far behind him.

"Xavier, follow me," she says. I follow her to her office, and as soon as I sit down, she dives right in.

"So we need to find an elective for you."

"I p-p-picked art, r-remember?"

Mrs. Tynes turns to her computer screen and starts clicking. She pauses, looks at me, and says, "Intro to Sewing is the only elective we have available."

"Huh?" I give Mrs. Tynes a look. There's gotta be something else. I picked *art!*

"I'm sorry, Xavier, that's the only elective I can put you in. The other ones have full class lists. Plus, sewing will still have you in the Arts track, like you selected."

What I wanna say is, Yo, Mrs. Tynes, this whole thing is your fault, but *I'm* the one who gets stuck with *sewing?* What I actually say is totally different.

"B-b-but I—"

"Mrs. Clark is a cool teacher; I'm sure you've heard that, right?"

No, I haven't heard of no Mrs. Clark, and even if I had, that don't change nothing about this screwup.

"I c-c-can't t-t-take s-something else?" I ask.

"Well, you have some core classes that I can't move," Mrs. Tynes says. "Especially with your first hour, when you'll likely be pulled to have speech therapy with Mr. G."

"S-s-so I'll have Mr. G-G?" I ask. Maybe that's the good news? I wanna be excited about it, but I'm still not feelin' no sewing class.

"Yes, looks that way," Mrs. Tynes says.

"B-b-but I don't s-s-sew," I say, trying to argue my way out.

"Oh, Mrs. Clark is great," Mrs. Tynes tells me. "Lots of knowledge and experience in the world of fashion. I've had tons of students say the same thing you just did, and then come and tell me how much they loved her class by the end of the year."

Mrs. Tynes is probably lying. The Aunt Kat in me calls her out.

"N-name one."

Mrs. Tynes looks confused.

"What—what do you mean?"

"A k-kid who liked it."

"I think all students who take sewing with Mrs. Clark are pleasantly surprised. And they all do well."

Riiiight.

"I'm going to print your new schedule so you can get to second hour," Mrs. Tynes says. "And for the record, Michael Sanchez took Mrs. Clark's elective here at Rosewood Middle and continued with her in high school. He interned in Paris and now is studying at the Fashion Design Institute in New York. Full scholarship."

I don't say anything. *One* guy, Mrs. Tynes, but whatever. She hands me my schedule, apologizes for the mix-up, and ends with a deal.

"Give it a try for two weeks, and then come see me, okay?" Mrs. Tynes says. "Neat socks, by the way. Way to rock your first day."

Seriously? I can't even hide my stank face. If I'm stuck in a sewing class instead of art, the socks are starting off as an epic fail.

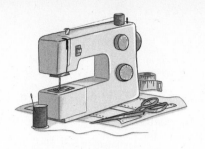

CHAPTER 8

"If God gave you a gift as golden as that,
you smile, say thank ya,
and no turning back!"

O ut of the eleven people in Intro to Sewing, exactly one of them is a guy.

Me.

When I trudge in and sit at one of the tables, all them girls give me a variety of looks that make me feel like I'm invading their sacred space. Shyanne from the bus scrunches up her face and whispers something to her friends. Even the teacher, the famous Mrs. Clark, raises an eyebrow like she's surprised I'm even in here.

Seventy-three seconds till the bell, and I'm praying some other dude will walk in and save me from looking completely dumb in this class.

Just before the ring, I can't believe who dashes into the class . . . red cornrow girl! She scans the room and then beelines for my table, where I was peacefully sitting

76

alone. She grabs the seat right next to me, which maybe isn't the worst thing in the world.

"Hey," she says. "You sew?"

My mouth is open and I'm *finally* about to find out her name when Mrs. Clark starts talking.

"Welcome to Introduction to Sewing," Mrs. Clark says. Her voice is deeper than I thought it would be, but also soothing, like Ma's. "I thought we were gonna have a perfect ten, but instead I see we're blessed with heaven's eleven."

She gives a small smile and winks at me when she says this, and some of the girls turn my way. I get the feeling they woulda preferred the perfect ten.

Mrs. Clark takes attendance, which obviously doesn't take long. First name she calls is Daysha Armstrong, which, it turns out, is Cornrow Girl. Daysha. That's a cool name. I make sure my brain remembers it.

Mrs. Clark drones on and on about the projects we'll be doing in this class, but I'm only half listening . . . until she calls me out.

"Mr. Moon," Mrs. Clark says, "what's the most important article of clothing you should have on every day?"

Man, she caught me off guard for real! I feel all eyes on me as I try and answer.

"Uhhhhh . . ." I hesitate, then say the worst possible answer. "U-underwear?"

A few of the girls giggle, and one in particular shoots me a look of disgust.

"Very important article of clothing," Mrs. Clark says with a chuckle. "But I guess I should've been more specific. What I'm looking for is an article of clothing that people will see."

"A shirt?" asks a girl at the table in front of me.

Mrs. Clark shakes her head.

"Pants?"

"A skirt?"

Mrs. Clark has a sly grin on her face, like she's the only one who knows a secret and absolutely loves that feeling.

"Socks."

We all look at her with giant question marks on our faces, and she laughs.

"That's right, ladies and gentleman, socks are one of the most important items you can put on every day. So that's where we'll be starting. Over the next few days, I'd like you to bring in pairs of socks that have holes. We'll be repairing them in class."

Well, I didn't think things could get any worse, but here we are. I'm stuck in a class with a bunch of girls fixing socks.

But then, while Mrs. Clark is answering questions

about the class and our big project, I start channeling my IFB—Inner Frankie Bell—and it hits me that I, Xavier Moon, am in a class *full of girls* and there are definitely some cuties in here. Frankie Bell would say, "If God gave you a gift as golden as *that*, you smile, say thank ya, and no turning back!"

I don't even realize I'm smiling until Mrs. Clark calls me out again. I get the feeling this is gonna be a normal thing for her.

"Ah, Mr. Moon, I believe we just discovered your area of interest," she says.

I have no idea what she was just talking about, or what area of interest I now have, but I nod and keep the grin on my face.

Whatever you say, Mrs. Clark. Just wait and see what Mr. Moon's gonna do!

CHAPTER 9

"The question is, what are you gonna do at twelve?"

I've recited the Scepter League Creed a thousand times in my head, so I know I got the words down. But when I have to say them in a rec center full of dudes who wanna get in the Scepter League like I do—when it counts for real, for real—I crash and burn.

"I will r-respect m-m-myself, m-my family, my s-s-school, and m-m-my c-c-community."

The rickety floor fans in the rec center gym are running at full speed, but my armpits are drenching my white dress shirt, and my tie feels like it's choking me. Mr. Donnel, the Scepter League director, is circling the room, listening to all us hopefuls recite the creed, and he passes by me right when I'm stuttering through the part about being a light for others.

I swallow hard and plop into my seat when Mr. Donnel tells us we can sit down.

"If you don't take those words seriously, you shouldn't be here," Mr. Donnel's voice booms. "This is not some poem you memorize for class; it is a higher way of living."

Mr. Donnel launches into the history of the Scepter League, which I already know from Frankie Bell. Some OGs back in the day wanted to start a club for young men to keep them out of trouble and help them be great. I go to loosen my tie, but my hand snaps down to my lap when Mr. Donnel's gaze shifts my way.

Pay attention, yo! I tell myself. I run my tongue over my braces, which I sometimes do when I'm nervous, and sit up straighter, like the dudes in the front of the room, behind Mr. Donnel.

The Scepter Leaguers.

Eighteen guys, every shade of brown there is, all dressed in white shirts, gold-and-green-striped ties, and green jackets with the Scepter League logo. #Clean. Julian's up there, too, which makes me feel a little bit better, even though it's not like he can help me or anything.

"Scepter League is for kings. When you walk down the hall at school, or down the street in your neighborhood, folks should be able to tell that you're different,"

Mr. Donnel says. "It's in the way you walk, how you dress, how you talk to people. How you shake hands, how you look someone in the eye."

I've heard this before—from my dad, from Frankie Bell, and sometimes their friends—but I don't know, there's something different about the way Mr. Donnel says it. Something strong and serious.

I swallow hard and wipe my palms on my black dress pants. The interview part is what I'm worried about the most. Doesn't matter how much I practice in my head, what comes out my mouth is never the same.

Two Scepter Leaguers talk next; one of them says he just graduated from high school and got accepted into Morehouse College, all the way in Atlanta.

"I never thought I would go to college, especially not one that was out of state," he says. "But the Scepter League gave me the tools to do my best in school and the confidence to make connections with influential people."

"I'm Ahmad," says the second guy. "I'm about to be a junior, and this summer I got to do a sports management internship with the Los Angeles Sparks. It was an amazing opportunity for real. They usually don't take you unless you're done with junior year, so it's a blessing I got to go."

We all clap when the guys take their seats. Mr. Donnel's two assistants speak next. They both were in the League when they were young and they talk about their lives now.

"Scepter League has lasting benefits," says Mr. Ford. "There's nothing like it."

"If you want the next level while you're young, this is it," adds Mr. Jones.

More applause. I lick my lips. I want the next level *right now.* And I know I'm ready. Once I get in, Frankie Bell can chill with all these socks. The League is gonna give me swag times ten!

"To be considered for the Scepter League, you must be a seventh grader or higher and hold a 2.6 GPA. You should also have two recommendation letters with you, and your essay describing why you want to be a part of the Scepter League."

I tighten my fingers around the black folder on my lap that holds my sixth-grade report card, essay, and letters from Mr. Joseph, one of my teachers from last year, and Mr. Hines, the counselor me and Shannon had to see after the thing with my parents. I look over and see that the dude next to me has a fancy green folder with his name in gold letters on the front. Dang! Mine looks like crap next to his.

"All right, gentlemen, we're gonna move on to the interview phase. You'll have a director and a few current Leaguers on your panel," Mr. Donnel tells us. "When we call your name, just come on back to the interview area and we'll chat. In following tradition, those selected to join the Scepter League will receive a Golden Scroll sometime on September twenty-ninth."

Mr. Donnel calls for Mike Parkinson, Christopher Lane, and JaQuan Perry, and I exhale a little. Latrell, who's sitting in front of me, turns around and whispers, "Yo, how many you think gonna get in?"

I shrug and let my eyes scan the room of all the hopefuls.

"It's probably like twenty dudes here," Latrell says.

Mr. Donnel never said nothing about taking only a certain number of guys.

"M-m-maybe everybody g-g-gets in," I say.

"Yeah." Latrell nods. "Yeah."

Latrell has a fresh cut, and I don't. Shannon said not to worry, that my hair looked fine. She lyin'. I don't think this nasty hair product she put in makes it any better.

"Yo," Latrell says, and scoots his chair toward me. "My dad said if I don't get in, I'm on punishment for the whole school year."

"Dang," I say. My dad isn't that hard-core, but it definitely sounds like something Frankie Bell would say.

Latrell pulls a brush from his pants pocket and runs it over his hair, even though he doesn't need to. Man, his tie looks better than mine, and his shoes are shiny black. He's trippin' off what his dad said, but I already know.

Latrell's gettin' in.

"Miles Jenkins, Xavier Moon, and David Cooper."

"Go kill it, bro," Latrell tells me, holding his fist out for dap. I nod and make my way to the back of the gym, where three interview areas have been set up.

"Mr. Moon, over here."

Great. Mr. Donnel's on my panel. I try to lock his hand in a death grip.

"Good to meet you, Mr. Moon; have a seat," Mr. Donnel says. He introduces the other guys on the panel. Two of them are freshmen, and one is an eighth grader. No Ju. One freshman asks me to tell them about myself.

"Umm, I'm Xavier, and I'm in s-seventh grade. I live with m-m-my s-s-s-sister and aunt."

I drop my eyes to my folder and stop talking. Then I remember I'm supposed to be looking them in the face, so my eyes pop back up.

"What are your hobbies?" the eighth grader asks. I recognize him from school. I wonder if he was nervous when he had to go through this last year. He don't look nervous at all right now.

Hobbies. Do I have any?

"I l-l-like video g-games and just b-being in my room."

I'm mentally kicking myself, because that sounds weak. What I wanna say is that my block is mad cool to watch from my bedroom window, and that sometimes I imagine it's a real-life video game. I wanna tell them that one day I'll design a game based on my neighborhood. I know for sure that's the stuff they wanna hear, but my brain keeps reminding me it'll take too long to get it all out.

Mr. Donnel takes over. "Mr. Moon, why are you interested in becoming a member of the Scepter League?"

In my mind, I rewind what my aunt said when she found out I wanted to join: *Boy, you too quiet for all that! There's other things for you.*

I open my mouth to tell this panel that I'm tired of being quiet, that green is already my favorite color, and that I gotta be in the Scepter League because I don't have anything else—not sports, music, art, cars, culinary skills, nothing. Well, there is one thing I do have. I wanna pull up my pant leg and show off my sock swag—black with gray and yellow zigzags. I wanna tell them I gotta be in the League before my dad gets out. He'll probably be a whole new dad, so I gotta be a whole new Xavier.

But I don't say any of that.

"My grandfather and u-uncle and d-d-dad were in it," I say. "I want to f-f-follow them."

Mr. Donnel nods, and they ask me a few more questions before shaking my hand again.

"Thank you, Xavier," he says. "We'll take your folder, and you're free to go."

They call Latrell's name as I walk toward the door. He's grinning before he even gets to his panel. I trudge from the gym to the lobby, and then outside for the long walk home in the blazing heat. I rip the tie off and stuff it in my pocket, trying not to replay every horrible detail of my interview.

Shannon's on the couch scrolling through her phone when I get home, and she goes in right away with the questions.

"How'd it go? I been texting Ju, but he's not telling me anything. Can't believe you're actually doing this!"

She's just like Aunt Kat; she won't say it, but she don't think I can get in. Not for real. I slump down on the couch and kick my feet out the jail-shoes.

"Hel-llloo!" says Shannon, glancing up from her phone. "How did it go?"

"Good," I tell her. *If good means I sucked!*

Shannon nudges me with her arm.

"Awww snap! My lil' bro 'bout to be a Leaguer!" she says, doing a mini dance celebration.

"Chill," I tell her.

"Ugh," Shannon says, looking at me like I'm an alien. "I hope you didn't have that funky attitude in there."

I ignore her and stare at this painting Aunt Kat has on the wall. Bunch of Black people dancing in a club.

"Oh, you not talking now? You in your feelings? You know, Walter came over here looking for you earlier; I can always go tell him you're home."

"Nah, Sh-Shannon, s-s-stop playin'!" Walter's perky butt is the *last* thing I need right now.

"Uh-uh." Shannon holds up a hand and cuts me off. "I got something for that mood."

She taps and swipes on her phone, and a few seconds later Pharrell's song "Happy" starts playing. I groan, which makes Shannon turn it up louder.

This song was my jam when I was a kid, and since our parents have been gone, Shannon plays it whenever she thinks I'm "in my feelings." Man, I always try and fight it, but I can't help smilin' when I hear this song.

"Got 'em!" Shannon jokes as I get up and dance like them people in Aunt Kat's picture.

It's not September 29, and I don't have that Golden Scroll yet, but tonight I'm gonna act like I do.

CHAPTER 10

"Must be somethin' 'bout pink."

Moonie,

    I got the finest woman in the city to finally go on a date with me on the day I wore a charcoal gray suit and a pastel pink shirt to one of my gigs. The fellas gave it to me over that shirt all night long, till she floated over when the band was breaking down and whispered something in my ear that I can't repeat to you. Must be somethin' 'bout pink.

                —Frankie Bell

This whole Inner Frankie Bell thing is freakin' amazing. All I gotta do is think more like him and do things the way he would. Today, it's all about confidence, just like he always says. I slide into school with some pink flamingo socks, which, not gonna lie, look like a hot pink mess. At first, I thought Frankie Bell was out his mind for sending them. But then I read his note, channeled my IFB, and was good to go.

The socks look a little off with my old gray shoes, but I hold my head high, shoulders back, and walk in like I own the school.

"Yo, you killin' my eyes! Are you serious right now?" Latrell clowns me, shielding his face while Adam cracks up.

"D-don't hate the s-s-swag," I tell him, holding my fist toward him.

"Where you gettin' those from anyway?" Adam asks.

"Classified," I say.

"Yeah, whatever," Latrell says. We walk to Innovation Lab and Latrell's talking about the Scepter League the whole time.

"You know they gonna be watching us until the twenty-ninth, right?" he says when we sit down at our table. "Teachers, eighth graders; it could be anyone!"

"Yeah," I say. Ju told me I gotta be on point at all times: no fights, no disrespecting teachers, no skipping class. He said sometimes high school Leaguers drop in on us.

"Man, y'all crazy," Adam says, shaking his head. "What are they, the secret service?"

"Nah, man, they gotta be sure we the right dudes for the League," Latrell says, then quickly adds, "Which we are."

Me and Latrell fist-bump again, and Adam rolls his eyes and changes the subject. We all know what's up with him, though: he doesn't have the grades for the Scepter League. To be honest, I'm surprised Latrell does. He's always playing around in class and brushing off his homework. Guess we'll see what happens.

Mad people say something about my socks when they come in the classroom; most of it ain't pretty. I act like it doesn't bother me either way. Ju told me that when they're making their decisions, Scepter Leaguers might ask teachers how we do in class, so I make sure I'm paying close attention to Mr. Kirk explain our project for the day.

"Look, it's bow tie guy!" Latrell whispers, laughing and pointing at the door. I follow his finger and see Mr. G standing in the doorway. I instantly know he's here for me. It's been a few weeks of school already, so I figured either they forgot to put me in speech the way they *forgot* to put me in art, or I didn't end up on Mr. G's caseload. I've seen him around, though, and Latrell's right; he's always wearing a bow tie. Today it's green with silver squiggly lines.

Mr. Kirk says, "Hello, Mr. Gerdino, who do you need?"

Mr. G has a clipboard in his hand but he doesn't even look at it.

"Let's just go with Mr. G," he says. "You slaughtered it, my man."

Mr. Kirk looks a little embarrassed. "Sorry about that. Mr. G, it is."

"Alrighty, so I gotta steal Jared and Xavier."

Mr. Kirk nods at us and we get our stuff to leave class. I always hate this part—everybody's eyes on me, wonderin' why I gotta leave class early.

"Yo, can I go, too, bow tie guy?" calls Latrell. People laugh, and I know some eyes have shifted off of me. Latrell better chill with all the goofiness if he wants to get in the League.

"Oh, I'm sure we'll chat sometime, big guy," Mr. G says to Latrell. "Just not right now."

Me and Jared follow Mr. G down the hall, and dude is actually whistling! We stop to pick up one more kid, and it turns out to be Daysha with the red cornrows, from my sewing class. We both look away a second after we make eye contact. I'm kinda confused about how we're in the same group for speech, cuz she definitely doesn't stutter like me.

"Welcome to my kingdom," Mr. G says, unlocking

his room and holding his arm out for us to walk in first. "Good news is, you won't need me to escort you next time."

"You like, you like, you like the beach?" Jared asks.

"I *love* the beach!" Mr. G says. "Can you tell?"

Jared nods. Mr. G has tan rugs, like sand, and his walls are a turquoise blue like water. He has beach pictures all over the small room, and palm tree plants in all four corners. It even smells like the beach, and I'm not sure how he did that. Definitely the coolest classroom in this school; bet the other teachers are jealous.

"Have a seat," Mr. G says, pointing to three orange chairs and a dark brown table. His chair's bigger, and it's green. "My sister did all the decorating, so if anything looks a little wild, it's her fault!"

I smile a little when he says that, cuz I'm thinking about Shannon. I'll probably have her decorate my crib one day. She really hooked up her room at Aunt Kat's house, with all this lavender flowery stuff. When we moved in, I didn't want no decorations. I didn't think we'd have to be there this long.

"I know I'm the new guy here," Mr. G says, "so how 'bout I share a little bit about myself to start?"

Jared nods and starts tapping on the table with his finger, which is his trademark. I shrug. Daysha doesn't say anything, but she has a look on her face like she literally would rather explode into flames as red as her hair than be here listening to Mr. G. Weird. She ain't like this in sewing class. In there, she's, like, into everything Mrs. Clark says.

Mr. G starts by telling us he moved here last year from Riverside, California, and he *totally* misses the beach. He and his sister both came so they could help take care of their mother, who got real sick out the blue. He said they all live together, and I think about me, Shannon, and Aunt Kat.

"My dad's in Japan," Mr. G says. "Never saw him too much, but he sends awesome photos! Some of them are in this room."

"You got you got a wife?" asks Jared. *Bro, so nosy!*

"I'm actually pre-married," Mr. G says. "What about you?"

Jared cracks up laughing and shakes his head. Daysha sucks her teeth. Mr. G looks at her and raises his eyebrows.

"What's the matter, Daysha?"

"Y'all dumb," she says.

"Why do you think that?" Mr. G asks. "We're just getting to know each other."

Daysha doesn't say anything. I can only imagine

what Aunt Kat would say if she was here. She might be screaming for Ms. Nixon to come back.

Mr. G tells us his favorite color (teal), food (fish tacos), holiday (Fourth of July), and sports team (Lakers). Then he hands us two colored sheets of paper. The yellow one says **All About** _____ and has a space for us to write our names.

"I want you to take a few minutes to fill these out," Mr. G says. "It will help the group—and me—learn a little more about you."

I scan the list and start filling in my answers. Favorite thing to do? Watch the block from my window. Favorite snack? Caramel popcorn (which I'm not supposed to eat with these braces, but whatever). Favorite color? Green. Word to describe me . . . ?

I look over at Daysha and she's got her lips poked out, staring at the paper like it did something to her. Jared's doing a combo of tapping his pencil and writing. Mr. G's filling out a sheet, too. After a few minutes, he puts his pencil down.

"Anybody wanna share?" Mr. G asks.

Crickets.

"Anything from your sheet," Mr. G says.

Tap tap tap from Jared.

"My favorite thing to do, my favorite thing to do is

play *Fortnite*," Jared blurts out. "I play every day. My mom hates it."

Mr. G laughs. "Moms are supposed to."

No one else wants to share, so Mr. G has us start on the next sheet, which is where we gotta write two goals we have for the school year. I think about mine in my head but feel like I'll jinx them if I write them down. *1. Stop stuttering! 2. Get into the Scepter League.* I figure number one's gonna be harder than number two, but hey, that's what Mr. G is here for. When Mr. G asks if we want to read our goals out loud, Jared says yeah. Daysha shakes her head. I almost do, too, but then I catch a glimpse of my pink socks and think about one more thing.

"M-m-my goal is t-to b-b-build up my s-s-sock game," I say.

"My kind of guy," Mr. G says with this big grin. He holds his hand up for a high five, but that's so kindergarten. Instead of leaving him hanging, I hold out my fist. He gets the hint.

Once Jared is done saying how he wants to make the track team and be the top *Fortnite* player in the world, Mr. G tells us our time is up for the day. I kinda want to stay a little longer, see if the socks combined with Mr. G can do some magic on my stuttering. But the bell rings and Daysha jumps up and grabs her stuff like it's a fire drill. I notice her papers on the table and they're both blank.

"Something on your mind, Xavier?" Mr. G asks. Jared and Daysha both look over at me.

"Um, n-nah," I say.

Head up, shoulders straight, I tell myself as I step out into the busy hallway.

Next time. I'll figure out what to say to Mr. G next time.

CHAPTER 11

*"Doors will open left and right when
you got CONFIDENCE, or as y'all
youngbloods say, swag."*

"**O**wwww!" I wince and grip the chair's armrests to keep my head from jerking.

"Hold still, buddy, we're almost there," Dr. Leonard, my orthodontist, says. "Sorry about that."

I'm normally not this pissed at my appointments, but Dr. Leonard is trippin' today. Not only does he keep poking me with the wire that he's tightening, but he also did *not* trim his nose hairs, and they're grossing me out.

Plus, out of *all* the days I could've had an appointment on, Aunt Kat chose today? TODAY?!

"Clear elastics today?" Dr. Leonard asks. That's what I've always gotten. But all that's gonna change now.

"Uh-uh," I say, my gums already throbbing from the tightening. "C-c-can I d-do green and g-g-gold?"

"Changing it up, huh?" Dr. Leonard chuckles. "I should have both those colors; I'll have Rhonda check for us."

Dr. Leonard lets me close my mouth while he asks his assistant about the elastics, and I lick my lips and sigh. The clock in this office says 8:22, which means I'm gonna miss first and second hour, maybe some of third if Dr. Leonard keeps moving like a sloth.

"Ain't no Scepter mess more important than yo' teeth!" Aunt Kat had said when I begged her to change my appointment from today. "They booked solid with snaggletooth kids, and this was the soonest I could get you in."

I told Aunt Kat I could wait, but she wouldn't budge. Said my teeth would shift back if I let too much time pass between appointments. I'm pretty sure that ain't true, but I'm also pretty sure it doesn't matter to Aunt Kat.

So here I am, stuck in a chair on September 29, the day we get our Golden Scrolls. Not only will I be late to school, but my mouth will also be mad sore. I bet if Frankie Bell was here, he woulda understood the importance of today and moved the stupid appointment.

"Lemme see 'em," Aunt Kat says when I walk out to the waiting room at 8:38. Instead of smiling, I bare my teeth like a wolf and she waves a hand at me.

"Boy, your drawls still in a bunch over this? Nice as your teeth look now?"

"Aunt Kaaaat," I groan. But she's already moved on to a conversation with Dr. Leonard about how my teeth are doing. I've never been so anxious to get to school, and Aunt Kat picks now to ask all these questions. I inch toward the door, fake-cough, look at my watchless wrist—anything to give Aunt Kat a hint.

"Ooops, someone has to get to school, I see." Dr. Leonard is the one who *finally* notices. "Let me not keep you folks. Xavier, good job. No broken brackets today."

"Thanks," I say, already turning the handle on the door.

I'm walking much faster than Aunt Kat, but I hear her chuckling behind me.

"Where's the fire?" she asks once we're in the car.

"Nowhere," I say.

"Mmm-hmm," she says.

Luckily, she doesn't say anything else until we get to school.

"So you gonna be a new man by the time you get home?" she asks me.

This time, I give her a real green-and-gold smile.

"I already am," I tell her.

"Lawd, you sound like Frankie Bell," she says, shaking her head.

I close the car door and walk toward the building, smoothing out my clothes. Latrell said we should dress nice today, so I have on some preppy-boy khaki shorts, a black polo, the black-and-neon-green socks, and my new Jordans. I've been saving the kicks for today, and it was super hard to wait.

After checking in at the office and getting a tardy slip, I walk to my locker with my heart pounding.

I am a young man of purpose, a descendant of kings. . . . I am disciplined, courageous, and confident. . . .

I spin my combination, take a deep breath, and open my locker.

Nothing.

I check under my math book and under some papers at the bottom of my locker. No Golden Scroll. Are you serious?

"Don't trip, they haven't done it yet," someone says behind me.

I whirl around and recognize a guy who was at the meeting at the rec center. He's tapping a bathroom pass against the lockers as he walks down the hall. I let out my breath in a rush, grab my math book, and head to class.

I don't see Latrell until lunch, and we smash burgers and fries even though we're on edge about the League.

"When y-y-you th-think th-th-they gonna do it?" I ask.

"Ion't know," Latrell says, licking ketchup from his

fingers. "When my brother got in, he got his Scroll in the morning."

"Man, they m-m-messin' with us," I say.

"Probably."

We check our lockers after lunch. Nothing. The rest of the afternoon goes the same way—dashing to my locker to look between classes. It's not until after sewing, my last class, that it finally happens.

The sewing classroom is far from the seventh-grade lockers, but I hear the commotion in the halls on my way there.

"Yeah BOI!" Latrell bounds over to me, and high above his head, he's clutching it.

A Golden Scroll.

I see a few other guys waving theirs around and dancing and recording themselves on their cell phones. I wish Aunt Kat could see this; it's a big deal.

"C'mon, bro, get to your locker!" Latrell nudges me in that direction before going to celebrate with some of the other guys who made it in. I catch Adam watching off to the side and he gives me a w'sup nod. I feel kinda bad for him.

But when I spin my combo and fling the door open, the smile slides off my face and it's really *me* I feel bad for.

Cuz there's no Golden Scroll in my locker.

CHAPTER 12

"If you ain't cryin' like a baby right now, I figure you got a chance."

Even though we had an unofficial bribe of hot Cheetos, Ju's big mouth musta slipped and told Shannon about my Scepter League epic fail. She hasn't said anything, but she's been being pathetically nice, like I'm fragile and about to fall apart.

Right now, she's standing at my door, interrupting my window time with a goofy look on her face.

"Me and Ju goin' to the movies; you wanna come?"

"No."

"Why not?"

"C-cuz I don't."

"You need to get out and do something fun."

I hold up my Switch, which was sitting beside me on the dresser. Shannon sucks her teeth but leaves me alone. . . .

Only for a few minutes.

"Bro, get up, you rollin' with us."

I look over and this time it's Julian standing in my doorway. Serious? His haircut is perfect, his clothes are perfect, and the Jays on his feet are perfect. Not gonna lie, seeing him standing there all Leagued up makes my eyes do that burning thing when tears are 'bout to escape. I blink hard. Can't go out like a punk, 'specially not in front of Ju.

"Nah, I-I'm g-good," I say, trying to keep the shakiness from my voice and the wetness out my eyes.

"Man, quit playin'!" Ju says. "I ain't ask you no questions; you comin' with us."

"Unless you wanna stay and help Aunt Kat clean out the kitchen cabinets," Shannon says with a smirk. I give her a dirty look cuz she know she fightin' dirty.

"Hurry up," Shannon laughs. "I wanna get there for the previews."

I roll my eyes and climb off the dresser. When Shannon and Ju leave my room, I try to decide what to wear. No way I'm gonna be on Ju's level, but I can definitely upgrade from the Star Wars pajama pants and T-shirt I'm in now.

It's been a week, and other than Shannon, nobody knows the truth. Dad was the hardest to avoid, cuz he called the same afternoon and the first thing he asked was, "So, what y'all doing to celebrate?" I have no idea how he even found out I was trying to get in the League; maybe Aunt Kat or Shannon said something. Traitors.

"We're just g-g-gonna do something here," I had said, which was technically true.

"Proud of you, man. Look at you, carrying on the tradition," Dad had said.

I wanted to ask him about the whole "tradition" thing. I mean, Dad was in the League, and where is he now? Locked up. Did the Scepter League not work for him? It for sure ain't working for me.

"Wish I could be there for your induction ceremony," he told me.

Well, Dad, I wish I could be there for the induction ceremony.

We ended up ordering pizza. The only thing I "carried on" was the pizza box to the table, and I couldn't even eat a slice cuz my mouth was still sore from my braces.

Frankie Bell sent me gold-and-green-striped socks, which are still under my bed. The whole thing is pretty embarrassing. All that's changed with me is that I've been looking dumber than usual in these stupid socks. I can't believe I really thought they would magically change everything. I should gather them all up—*without* washing them—and send them back to Frankie Bell.

When I slump downstairs, Shannon and Ju are stand-ing in the kitchen talking to Aunt Kat. I wonder if she knows I didn't get in, cuz she hasn't said anything about it either. Oh shoot, if Aunt Kat knows, does that mean Frankie Bell knows? My heart drops all the way down to the plain white socks I'm wearing.

"You look great," Shannon says.

I roll my eyes. *A hoodie and jeans, Shannon?* What-ever. She's just being nice.

"You might wanna fix your face, Moonie," Aunt Kat says. "Right now, you lookin' like you much rather stay here with me."

I fight the urge to roll my eyes and instead plaster on a fake-ish smile.

Aunt Kat grills Ju about what time the movie starts and ends, and when we should be home. It's actually a miracle she's letting us ride with him, cuz at first she didn't trust him driving. He finally convinced her to ride with him to the post office once, and that changed her mind. She came home shocked; said, "That fool drives better than me!" It's actually not hard to believe that.

I start feeling better when we go outside to the car. Ju might be in the League, but his car is a piece of crap. It's an old gray Ford Taurus with a ton of dents and scratches, and when he starts it up, it sounds like one of Frankie Bell's dramatic coughs.

"Xavier, where ya going? Can I come?"

I turn and see Walter barreling down the sidewalk on his bike. Great.

"Not this time, Walter," Shannon says, which surprises me. He came over the other day, and when I said I didn't wanna go outside, Shannon sent him up to my room! Shady move.

"We can ride bikes when you get home!" Walter calls. I give him a half-hearted wave. It's gonna be nothin' but window time later.

Ju plays music while we drive, and since I'm in the back seat, the scratchy sound of his blown-out speakers pounds my eardrums. I stare out the window and don't say a word the whole drive. Shannon and Ju don't say anything to me, either. I know what this is about. I'm the third wheel to make sure they don't try nothing in the nasty back seat of this wreck. Aunt Kat probably made them take me.

It takes us a while to find a parking spot, but when we finally do, I'm the last one to climb out the car. Shannon looks like she wanna say something to me, but doesn't. She's smart like that.

"I can p-pay for m-myself," I say once we get up to the counter and Ju asks for three tickets.

"Aight, that's wassup." Ju nods, telling the clerk two tickets instead.

This time Shannon elbows me and whispers through clenched teeth, "Why you actin' all stank?"

"I'm not!" I whisper.

Shannon makes her eyes big and points at Ju, who's still turned around, and then at me. Then she points to her temple, like, *Think, Xav!*

And that's when I feel dumb. Again. Does she mean I'm embarrassing her in front of Ju? Like I care! I didn't even wanna come! Then it hits me. Maybe she means I still have a chance to get into the League. Maybe Ju's trying to help me out. Maybe he'll report something good to Mr. Donnel and all them.

Ju buys popcorn and soda for him and Shannon to share, and I get an overpriced box of Whoppers. We make it to our seats right before the previews, which Shannon gets way too excited about. I'm on one side of her and Ju's on the other. I try not to notice when his arm snakes around her ten seconds into the first preview.

The movie is aight: typical hero-saves-the-world kind of thing. But what got me is something the main character says to the girl he's in love with, but who doesn't give him the time of day until he's saving her stupid life: "I've always been the man; you not seeing it didn't change anything."

That's pretty much me, unseen by everyone. Only I'm not a hero, and I don't feel like faking it anymore. Being regular Xavier was so much easier.

Frankie Bell is just gonna have to get used to it.

CHAPTER 13

"Whatcha waitin' for, chest hair
to appear?"

"**U**mmm, hello? You still here?"

"Huh?"

My head swivels from the group of guys who just sauntered into the park to Daysha, who's got her hands out for the ball. We're on the court and she's shooting, like, a million free throws. As we were getting off the bus today, Daysha asked me if I wanted to hang out. I was all excited, too! Now I see I'm just her ball boy, feeding her the rock so she can put up more shots.

"S-s-sorry," I say, trotting off to grab the ball. Can't help glancing over at those guys again. They're eighth graders, and most of them are in the League. One of them looks over at us and nudges the dude next to him.

"Wassup, Daysha!" the first guy calls. She waves but doesn't say anything.

"Wanna run a game with us?" the guy yells over.

"Nah, maybe later," Daysha calls back. She looks at me and motions for the ball.

I toss it to her, and she flips it twice, sets her feet, and launches a shot that touches nothing but net. I grab the ball and pass it to her. She sinks another. Those guys are watching us—*her*, really—but it's like she doesn't even notice.

I'm the complete opposite. I keep imagining them all laughing at me cuz they know I'm the loser who didn't make it in the League. Latrell told me that out of all the new Leaguers, only three were seventh graders. Man, why couldn't there have been four?

"That's a hundred," Daysha says after sinking her last shot.

"For real?" I haven't really been counting.

"Yup." Daysha dribbles through her legs. "I usually make two hundred, but I got all this science homework. You want a turn?"

Daysha is about to pass the ball to me, but I shake my head. No use humiliating myself. Basketball is definitely not my thing. It seems like nothing is my thing.

"When d-d-does the s-s-s-season start?" I ask her.

"Tryouts in November," she says. "I have to make the team. No matter what."

Something about the way she says "No matter what" is a painful reminder of my epic fail situation.

"What if you d-don't?" I ask. It's selfish, but I'm kinda hoping somebody else will get their dreams snatched away.

"If I don't what?"

"M-make the t-team."

Daysha bounces the ball and looks like she never considered not being on the team.

"I'd talk to the coaches and make sure they know they made a mistake," she finally says. "And then I make the team."

Daysha's near the three-point line, and when she shoots, I don't think it's gonna go in. But it banks off the backboard and slides into the net.

"Gotta go," she says, grabbing her own rebound this time. "See ya."

"Bye."

Can girls have swag? Cuz if they can, Daysha *definitely* has it. I watch her talk to the other guys for a few minutes before she leaves, dribbling the ball the whole time.

I think about what she said, that she would tell the coaches they made a mistake, and that gives me an idea.

I take a deep breath and walk over to those eighth-grade guys, trying to look like I ain't got a care in the world. I'm about to say w'sup, but one of them beats me to it. Now that I'm closer, I see it's the dude who was on my panel at the info meeting.

"Ay, you the sock boy, right?" he says with a grin. His eyes drift down, but all I got on are plain white socks. That's what I've been wearing lately.

"W'sup." I nod, not answering his question.

"Yo, you know her?" he asks. Takes me a few seconds to realize he's talking about Daysha.

"Yeah," I say.

"Which street she live on?"

I decide to channel my IFB before answering this one.

"Sh-she lives b-b-b-by me," I say. It's probably not the answer he wants, but I'm not about to just tell them where her house is.

Two of the guys shake their heads and keep shooting around. The guy who was on my panel asks, "You tryna get in this game or something?"

I shake my head.

"I'm tryna g-get in the League," I say. "Y'all m-m-messed up."

Neither one of us was expecting me to say that, but there it is.

"I mean, you can try again next year," he says with a shrug. "Or the year after that."

I stare at him, trying to figure out if he's low-key blazing me. I don't get a chance to find out, cuz he heads over to his friends before I can say anything else.

Okay, so maybe this wasn't the best move. Who are they, anyway? Just members. Talking to them ain't gonna change nothing. I gotta talk to somebody else.

I race home and run up to my room. I hear Aunt Kat yelling at me, but I just say "Yes, ma'am!" and keep moving. I reach under my bed until I feel the green-and-gold socks. And even though they don't match what I'm wearing *at all,* I put them on and dash downstairs.

"Be right back, Aunt Kat!" I call, racing out the front door.

"Boy, you must got the devil on yo' tail!" she yells behind me.

Maybe I do. . . .

The walk to the rec center seems longer than last time. By the time I get there, sweat is dripping down my back and I'm breathing heavy. I try not to think about the fact that I'm gonna have to walk all the way home, too.

I will carry myself with dignity and honor in all situations. . . .

The Scepter League Creed is cemented in my brain even though I'm not in, so I wipe my forehead, pull the door open, and walk inside.

The rec center smells how it always does, like floor wax and sweat, with sounds of squeaky sneakers, basketballs thumping, whistles blowing, and trash-talking. I should definitely tell Daysha to come here to practice her game.

I head straight for the water fountain in the lobby and take huge gulps that trickle like icicles down my throat. The water's probably the coldest thing in the building. I stand up and swipe at the water dribbling down my chin. Not a good look. I'm walking toward the gym when a girl at the front desk stops me.

"Are you here for open gym? You need to sign in," she says, pointing to a clipboard on the desk.

"I-I-I'm l-looking for M-Mr. Donnel," I say.

"You have an appointment?" the girl asks. I shake my head.

"Well, sign in anyway, and hold on," the girl says, picking up the phone.

I write my name super neat on the paper and listen to the girl's conversation.

"Hey, Jada, is Mr. Donnel in his office? He busy? Yeah, okay, I think one of his Scepter League kids is here." The girl's eyes drift down to my T-shirt, which has a huge water spot on the front. The look on her face crushes my soul.

"You can head back," the girl tells me. "His office is in the gym."

I tell her thanks and walk into the gym, where the noise instantly goes from muffled to loud. Multiple games are going on at once and the same rickety fans are just moving warm air around. I recognize a few kids from school on my way to where two offices are.

"Come on in!" a voice says when I knock on the cracked door that has GREGORY DONNEL, DIRECTOR on it.

The door squeaks when I push it open, and Mr. Donnel looks up from the newspaper he's holding. He immediately knows I'm not one of his Leaguers, and I can tell he doesn't remember me from the meeting or the interview either.

"How can I help you, young man?" he asks. Yo, how can somebody be friendly and scary at the same time?

"Um, h-h-hi," I say. "I'm Xavier M-Moon, a-and I wanna t-talk to you about the S-S-S-Scepter League."

"Have a seat," Mr. Donnel says, pointing to a chair across from his desk. When I sit down, he asks, "You read the paper, Mr. Moon?"

"Huh?" I say, but then quickly try to fix it. "I m-m-mean, n-n-n-no, s-sir."

"Hmmm." Mr. Donnel nods, folding the paper and putting it down. "Last thing I do before I leave work every day; been doing it for years. Something special about feeling a nice crisp paper in your hands. It beats swiping and tapping for everything."

I nod, cuz I have no clue what to say right now. But Mr. Donnel's starting to sound scary familiar. I guess once you get in the League you start making weird, random comments and speaking in riddles to confuse everyone else.

Mr. Donnel finally breaks the awkward silence.

"I'm glad you're interested in the League, but I gotta let you know that we're already inducting a group of young men for the fall."

"I kn-know. You interviewed m-me."

Mr. Donnel cocks his head to the side and studies me.

"What you say your name was?"

"Xavier Moon."

"Xavier Moon," he repeats to himself. Wow. I'm pathetically forgettable. "You Roy Moon's boy?"

"Y-y-yes."

"Small world!" Mr. Donnel smiles big. "I remember your daddy from elementary. How's he doing?"

"G-good," I say. There's another awkward silence as it probably hits Mr. Donnel that my dad made it into the League and I didn't.

"Well, Xavier, our next induction will take place next fall."

I nod, and I almost stand up and leave without saying

anything else. But I think of Daysha's hundred shots and I lean forward a little, look Mr. Donnel in the eyes.

"I h-heard you can g-g-get in during s-s-spring," I say. Latrell told me that, but judging by Mr. Donnel's face when I mention it, I'm not sure that's true.

"It is *extremely* rare that we induct young men in the spring," Mr. Donnel says. "There are great benefits to having a full year to devote to only one set of new Leaguers."

"S-s-so it's rare, b-but you do it," I say, a question inching into my voice.

"We've done it before, yes," Mr. Donnel tells me. His fingers tap the paper. "If we have promising young men present themselves as candidates."

"I w-wanna know why," I say.

"Pardon me?"

"Why you d-d-didn't pick me," I say, then add, "s-s-sir."

Mr. Donnel doesn't answer right away, just stares at me hard, like he's never gotten this question before.

"Leadership, Education, Service, and Character," Mr. Donnel finally says. "Those are the pillars on which the Scepter League is based. Think of it like the four legs of that chair you're sitting on. If one leg is missing, you'd be off balance. If two are gone, you're pretty much on the floor."

Okaaay. I know all about the pillars; they're drilled into my brain just like the creed is. Mr. Donnel pauses for minute.

"When we consider a young man for membership in the League, we are looking for him to embody those pillars."

I run my tongue over my braces. Is this dude saying I don't have the pillars?

"Now, I'm not saying you don't have the pillars," Mr. Donnel continues, like he's reading my mind. He puts his hands up as if to stop me from popping up from this stupid old chair and slamming my way out the office—which is what I feel like doing.

"In fact, if I remember correctly, your academics were pretty solid, and your references spoke highly of your character," Mr. Donnel says. "We were also impressed by your volunteer work at the lower school."

I smile to myself, so glad that I signed up to do art with kindergartners a few times last year, even though I really didn't want to. Guess it paid off!

But then there's silence, and I realize Mr. Donnel's missing one.

Leadership???

So I'm not a leader? Wow. My heart thumps faster and I don't really know how to feel. Angry? Sad? Like a loser? Frankie Bell always says the world needs follow-ers, but it's better not to be one.

I'm *not* a follower!

"You m-m-made a m-mistake," I tell Mr. Donnel. I'm kinda shocked when the tiniest grin crosses his face and he nods his head a little.

"Well, son," Mr. Donnel says, picking up his paper again, "you got about four months to prove that."

CHAPTER 14

*"Pretend you're Denzel, or
whoever else them little girls whoop
and holler over nowadays."*

Ms. Yates in Language Arts is trippin' today.

She passes out old newspapers and tells us to pick a news article and write an alternate story idea from what's already on the page.

"For example," Ms. Yates explains, holding up a page, "this is a story about the search for a new president of Hamilton Community College. Your new story idea might be that the old president decided he really wanted to be a balloon artist and travel across the country, from carnival to carnival."

Some kids boo Ms. Yates and clown her for being so corny.

"Well, I'd hate for your *grade* to be corny," Ms. Yates says, unfazed. "So the point is to be creative."

She passes out pages, and as soon as I glance down at the black-and-white photo on mine, I know right away that the group of smiling guys in the photo are wearing green blazers. The article is from 2001 and the title reads "Popular local group organizes a toy drive."

Seriously? It's like the Scepter League is haunting me! I look up at Ms. Yates to see if she did this on purpose and is now laughing hysterically, but nah. She's circling the room helping kids at another table.

I scan the names listed under the photo, but don't see my dad's mentioned. I read the article to see if it says anything about him, and try to remember what year he was even in high school.

Ms. Yates says time's up while I'm still reading, so I scribble out a pretty weak story idea.

"I hope you've got some good thoughts down, because we'll spend the rest of class actually writing your revised stories."

Everybody's groaning, and Ms. Yates only smiles.

"Ahhh, music to my ears," she says. "Sounds of creativity filling my classroom!"

I can't really focus on the assignment. I keep staring at that picture and thinking about what Mr. Donnel said. It still bothers me, but now it also makes me feel . . . different. Like, this dude rejected me, but it's like he gave me a challenge, too. He said I have four months; that means something, right? All I gotta do is figure out what to do.

It's not until lunch that I get my great idea.

"I see you lookin' over there," Adam says after we sit down and start eating. Latrell's sitting at a table with the other Leaguers, not with us. He does that a lot now, and I'm not gonna lie; sometimes it feels real awkward to even be around Latrell. I mean, he's still my boy and all, I guess. It's just . . . he got in, and I didn't.

"Nah," I say. "I w-w-was j-just thinking. W-w-we should s-start our own thing."

"Whatchoo mean?" Adam asks.

"L-l-like, our own club."

Adam frowns. "Can we even do that?"

"We can d-do wh-whatever we want," I tell him.

Mr. Donnel thinks I'm not a leader? Hey, maybe I'm not. But I'm gonna turn into one and prove him wrong. I'm gonna start my own club and do something epic—something to get us in the paper, like the Scepter Leaguers I just read about. Mr. Donnel will see it and be like, *Dang! How did we let that young man get away?*

Yeah, Mr. Donnel. How did you?

"You gonna eat those?"

Adam's eyeing my tater tots. So unfocused.

"Nah," I say, sliding the tray toward him. He eats 'em like they're the best thing ever.

"A c-c-cooking club?" I ask.

"You crazy." Adam shakes his head. "Nobody's gonna join that."

I shrug, thinking about Shannon, who goes hard for the cooking club at her school. I'm about to suggest a drawing club, but Adam interrupts me.

"How 'bout a gaming club?" he says. "Where people get together and, you know, game."

I start to smile. I can get down with that.

"Yeah," I say as the lunch bell rings. "That c-c-could work."

We just have to create a game like *Fortnite* that'll take off and make millions. I'm hyped and ready to get to work on the club, but the day drags by until it's time for my last class. Intro to Sewing.

Sewing has been . . . interesting. I never thought I'd be spending so much time needle-and-threading old socks with a bunch of girls, but the truth is, it does have its perks.

For example, this girl Alyssa sits at the table behind me and is always talking to her friend, Tori, about what happens in other classes, who texted who what, and who they think is cute. I basically just pretend not to listen, but listen. That's how I found out Alyssa likes Latrell. At first, Adam and Latrell clowned me when they found out I had to take sewing as my elective, but that all changed once I started giving them the scoop on pretty much all the seventh-grade girls at Rosewood.

"Today, we'll be working on a simple apron pattern," Mrs. Clark says. "When I call your table, come on up and pick your material."

Daysha practically jumps up from her seat when Mrs. Clark points to our table. I take my time. The front table has different bolts of fabric—fancy terms we gotta know in this class. There's an army fatigue one, a pinky sparkly one, leopard print, purple polka dot, and a brown one with mixing bowls and rolling pins and cookies all over it. That's the one Daysha goes for. To be honest, that's low-key the one I wanted, too, but I don't wanna look like I'm copying her. I bet everybody in here expects me to grab the army fatigue fabric, so I decide to change it up, give 'em something to talk about. Plus, what do I need with an apron anyway? This is going straight to Shannon.

"Xavier, your favorite color is purple?" asks this girl Carlita. She's not even tryna hide her condescending snicker.

"Me? N-nah," I say, super cool. "M-m-makin' this f-for my s-s-sister."

"Oh," says Carlita.

"Aww, that's so sweet!" says Alyssa.

Some of the other girls look over and go "Awwww!" too. And bingo! I exist now.

"Do you like this class?"

"Must be weird to be the only guy, right?"

Those questions came from Tori and Shyanne. So glad I was memorizing names when no one was talking to me; when I think about it, that's such a Frankie Bell thing to do. Which reminds me. I gotta start wearing the socks again tomorrow.

"It's aight," I say, answering both questions.

Mrs. Clark shows us the pattern for the apron and how to cut the fabric. A few of the girls mess up and have to start over with new fabric, but not me. I can tell Mrs. Clark's a little irritated.

"Ladies, please make sure you're paying attention to your work," she says, walking around the room. "Tomorrow, we move to the sewing machines, and we're gonna have to be very focused."

"We should just sew their mouths shut," Daysha says under her breath. I know she's talking about Alyssa and Tori, who talk all class long. I snicker. Daysha shoots me a look that makes me shut up super quick.

"I take this seriously," she says.

"I know," I say. "Me t-t-too." It's kind of a lie, but whatever. I mean, how is it fair that Daysha has *two* things—basketball and sewing? Some of us are just trying to find one!

"Ummm, riiiight," Daysha says, rolling her eyes.

I guess that extra attitude and eye roll messed her up, though, cuz when Mrs. Clark comes around to our table, she points out an area where Daysha cut too deep.

"The good news is that we can fix that pretty easily," she says, showing Daysha how.

"Good job, Xavier," Mrs. Clark tells me before moving on. I love the tiny bit of surprise in her voice. Daysha tries to pretend that she's not looking at my cutout, but I see her. In my mind, I'm thinkin', *I will be a man who lights the way for others.*

Man, Mr. Donnel don't even know what's 'bout to happen. He wants a leader? Okay. I'm already a leader to all these *girls* in a freakin' sewing class!

I'm still on a high when I get home, and since Aunt Kat's car isn't parked on the street or in the back, I do something extra bold. After making sure Shannon's not here, I head to the basement.

The steps creak as I go down, and I freeze, even though no one's in the house to hear me. I suck my teeth, tell myself to quit being stupid, and walk down there like it's my room.

The basement is dark, like always; the only light comes

from the storm window, but that's enough for me. I grab Frankie Bell's hat off his bed, prop it on my head the way he would, and check myself out in the mirror.

"Ohhhh, n-n-now you w-want me in the L-League?" I pretend I'm talking to Mr. Donnel and laugh. "Well, I g-g-gotta check my c-calendar."

I laugh again, this time all maniacal, but then I get this weird feeling. I look around, cuz it feels like somebody's watching me. I say a few more things to the mirror, aka Mr. Donnel, then I put the hat back where it was and race up the stairs. Yo, I swear on everything I love, that basement feels like magic and I get a little more Frankie Bell swag each time I go down there. I'm gonna need every bit of it to make this club thing work and take me right on into the League.

CHAPTER 15

"I'm everywhere I need to be."

The next morning, I wake up with a jerk, and my heart's racing, like somebody's in the room. I blink and look around, and it's still kinda dark. I pretty much have a mini heart attack when I see Frankie Bell leaning against my dresser, staring at me with a toothpick in his mouth.

"Don't wet your britches, now," Frankie Bell says, chuckling. "'Bout time you woke up."

"H-h-h-how—?" I start talking, but then stop. *What is going on?* I was sneaking around in Frankie Bell's space last night and now he shows up in my room, out the blue?

"Get dressed, Moonie," Frankie Bell says, pushing off my dresser and checking his watch. "Think you can pull it together in twenty minutes? Wearing something half-way presentable?"

I open my mouth again to ask Frankie Bell when he got here, why he's here, and where we're going, but he's already in the hall and then creaking downstairs.

I swing my legs out of bed and stumble to my closet. My heart's beating fast as I look through my clothes. Frankie Bell was wearing a suit. I hope that's not what he wants me to wear, cuz all I got is that black one. I probably shouldn't wear jeans either, so I grab some slim-fit khakis. Dang, they're a little short, but I figure if I wear a pair of cool socks, it won't matter. The socks might actually make Frankie Bell go easy on me. I swipe deodorant under my arms, pull on a red sweater over my T-shirt, and pick the red-and-white-striped socks he sent just a few days ago. My white Converse low-tops are dingy, but it's the best I got right now.

I pull the comforter up on my bed and head to the bathroom to brush my teeth. On my way, I knock on Shannon's door and crack it open. She's under the covers knocked out and snoring. A part of me wants to shake her awake so she can save me. The other part tells me to just take it like a man.

When I get downstairs, Frankie Bell's sitting at the table reading a newspaper (yo, what is it about papers?) and Aunt Kat's in the kitchen, fussing as she makes breakfast. Frankie Bell's doing a good job of ignoring the mess out of her. He has on these reading glasses that make his eyes look bigger, and he peers over the top of them when I come in the room. He scans me from head to toe before grunting and going back to his paper. I'm guessing I passed?

"Got me up at the crack of dawn like I'm workin' in the big house," Aunt Kat says, bringing out biscuits, grits, eggs, and sausages.

"Nobody asked you to cook for an army, Kat," Frankie Bell says. He takes off the glasses and starts piling his plate. "Ummph ummph, but I'm sho' glad ya did, old gal."

Aunt Kat purses her lips, trying to keep the smile in, but it doesn't work. I look away before she can see me, with a grin of my own.

"Wh-wh-where we g-goin'?" I ask Frankie Bell.

"Yeah, Frankie Bell, where you *think* you takin' him?" Aunt Kat asks.

"Gotta see a horse about a dog," Frankie Bell says, winking at his sister. Aunt Kat huffs into the kitchen and returns with a pitcher of orange juice, which she slams down pretty close to Frankie Bell. He pours a glass like it's nothing and goes on eating.

"Always so secretive," she says. "Now you got him into all this League business and the saga continues."

I freeze. Why she gotta mention that? I'm expecting Frankie Bell to start grilling me with questions about why I didn't make it, but he's quiet. He finishes his food before me, and I hold my breath and stop chewing when he goes down to the basement after he takes his plate to the kitchen. I'm trying to remember if I left a light on, or if I moved anything while I was down there. The biscuit I'm chewing gets stuck in the back of my throat and I start coughing. Aunt Kat shakes her head and pours me a glass of orange juice.

"Takin' you outta here to be around God knows what kinda foolishness," Aunt Kat mutters.

I'm taking my plate to the kitchen when he clumps upstairs with a bag in his hand. He doesn't yell at me, so I guess I'm okay.

"We'll be back tonight," he tells her. "Might be late."

Frankie Bell pushes me toward the door, but I hear him thank Aunt Kat for breakfast.

"Exquisite as always, my dear," he says. I peek over my shoulder and see Aunt Kat trying to hide her smile again. Man, I gotta learn how to make her do that!

I climb into the front seat of Frankie Bell's car and it's completely different from Ju's ride. Leather seats, high-tech dashboard, and most importantly, it's clean. Aunt Kat watches us from the door but shakes her head when Frankie Bell waves goodbye.

"That woman been a mother hen forever," Frankie Bell says as he reverses out the driveway. "I give her a hard time, but that's my baby."

"D-d-d-do you h-have a sh-show?" I ask.

"No," he says. "We got a few days off."

"Then wh-where—"

"Questions, questions," Frankie Bell cuts me off, then chuckles. "I'm takin' you to see the future."

The future. Okay. Aunt Kat and Frankie Bell musta gone to the same school to learn how to talk in code. Like, what are you even saying? I guess I should be happy he's not going on and on about how disappointed he is that I didn't get into the League.

Frankie Bell pops in one of his group's CDs and I stare out my window, watching the block pass by. It's still kinda dark out, but when we go by the playground, I see a figure moving on the court. Not 100 percent sure, but something tells me it's Daysha. That girl is intense!

"You a lot like your grandfather," Frankie Bell says as he merges onto the highway. "Always watching and thinking. He wouldn't do nothing till he thought it over a million times."

Frankie Bell doesn't say it like it's a bad thing. He tells me a story about how they were both interested in buying a car around the same time, and how competitive things got.

"Me? I looked at two cars and bought the first one cuz it just felt right. Didn't ask a lot of questions; just bought it. Beat my big brother. He took a whole month! Looking under hoods, talking sellers to death about the car. If a perfect stranger was driving the same kinda car he was interested in, he'd walk right up to them and ask what they liked about the car." Frankie Bell smiles at the memory. "Yeah, I rode him hard that month, but wouldn't you know, less than a year later, my 'feels right' car was in the junkyard and Arthur's lasted him almost a decade!"

"I d-d-don't really r-remember him," I tell Frankie Bell.

"What was you, 'bout two, three when he passed?" Frankie Bell sighs and shakes his head.

"Y-y-yeah. It w-was my m-m-mom's fault, right?"

"What?"

The car jerks a little when Frankie Bell looks over at me.

"Is that what somebody told you?"

I shrug.

"Look at me, Moonie," Frankie Bell says. "Whoever said that is mistaken. Lemme guess. Your aunt Nadine and your aunt Crystal?"

I nod.

"Th-they said sh-she had done s-s-something b-b-bad and he was y-yelling at her when it happened."

Frankie Bell cusses under his breath and I see him grip the steering wheel tighter.

"Moonie, your granddaddy was fussing at *them:* your grandmother and aunties. They was ganging up on your mama, as usual, and he had enough. But regardless, he had other medical conditions, things he never told any of us. As meddlesome as they were, they didn't cause his heart to stop. Was his time to go. When it's my time, I wanna rest easy, knowing all y'all have found your path in life. Knowing maybe I helped direct you to it in some small way."

"H-h-how d-did you know wh-what your p-p-path was?" I ask.

"The girls was the ones supposed to have piano lessons," Frankie Bell tells me, "but I would follow behind them, listening to everything their teacher said. One day, my sister Dorothy decided she was gonna skip her piano lesson cuz she wanted to play instead. Well, I walked on over to Miz Reed's house all by myself, told her I was gonna do the lesson for Dorothy. I sat at that piano and played better than all four sisters combined!"

I think this is the most me and Frankie Bell have ever talked, and I feel like we could probably talk for days to get through all I wanna know. At the same time, I want to just take in what's already been said, to think about what my path is gonna be.

Turns out "the future" is not right around the corner, cuz I fall asleep and wake up a few hours later to Frankie Bell shaking my shoulder.

"Rise and shine, Moonie," he says. "You was out cold, boy. Left me alone with all my thoughts."

I blink and stretch, trying to figure out where we are and why Aunt Kat was so worried about it. I see a sign that says CENTRAL STATE UNIVERSITY. Wait. A school? Frankie Bell woke me up early on a Saturday to go to a school? Maaaan.

"Welcome to my alma mater, boy," Frankie Bell says with a grin. He opens his car door and cool air rushes inside. He climbs out and stretches, and I do the same.

It's October, so the air is that mix of warm and cool. Feels good.

"Let's walk," Frankie Bell says.

The campus is in the middle of nowhere, spread out and with trees and stuff. I see signs everywhere that say WELCOME ALUMNI! and HOMECOMING WEEKEND, and lots of people are just strolling around, like me and Frankie Bell. As corny as it sounds, I can feel, like, excitement floating around as we walk.

"Y-y-you w-went here?" I ask.

"Mighty class of '71," Frankie Bell says, a smile spreading across his face. He seems to walk even taller, but I'm like, *Dang! He's old as dirt!*

Frankie Bell points at different buildings as we walk and scratches his head when he sees stuff that's new.

"Well, they sho' ain't have that last time I was here," he says. The more we walk, the more people we see. A parade starts and then there's music and cars and everybody wearing maroon and yellow. Frankie Bell watches it all from behind his shades, like he knows he's the coolest one around.

"Now, I know that ain't Frank!" somebody calls. We turn around and see two old guys strolling over to us. The one in the front slaps hands with Frankie Bell and they hug.

"In the flesh, you know it best!" Frankie Bell says.

"You ain't told nobody you was gonna be here, baby!" says the second guy.

"Element of surprise, you know how I do." Frankie Bell grins. "How you hangin', Monroe?"

"Can't complain," says the guy named Monroe. "What about you, baby? Heard you was on the road again."

Frankie Bell shrugs and grins, holding his hands up like, *What can I say?* Both guys laugh, and the first one shakes his head.

"I'm tryin' to figure out how anybody even still wanna hear yo' old—"

Frankie Bell coughs loudly and nods his head toward me. "This here's my nephew, Moonie."

"Well, hey, Moonie," says Monroe. He holds out his hand and I shake it.

"Hi, s-sir," I say, hating my stutter even more in front of them.

The first guy shakes my hand, too.

"Well, if you any relation to him"—the guy jerks a thumb at Frankie Bell—"I'm sure you already done heard it all and yo' ears still bleeding."

"If he bleeding after me, he won't have no eardrums after you," Frankie Bell says. He points at the men. "That's Clyde, and that's Monroe. My brothers from some other mothers."

"Nice to meet ya, youngblood," Clyde says. "How you like it so far?"

"It's c-c-cool," I say.

"Yeah, you got him dressed right, Frank," Monroe says with a wink.

"I ain't do a thing," Frankie Bell says proudly. "He did that on his own."

"So we got a legacy on our hands," Clyde says, thumping me on the back. I stand a little straighter, cuz now I realize these guys are Frankie Bell's frat brothers from

138

way, waaaay back in the day. Frankie Bell and his friends keep talking and laughing for what seems like forever, and I tune them out after a while. All I can see is my empty locker and Latrell's smile slipping away like an icicle in July when he realized he was the only one with a Golden Scroll in his hand.

"Well, I guess we gonna head over to the homecoming game," Frankie Bell says. "Let him see as much as possible, you know."

"Yeah, y'all go on and check that out," Monroe says. "We'll see you later, right?"

"You know it," Frankie Bell says.

"Harris over there working security," Clyde says. "Make sure you look for that nappy gray Afro."

The men laugh again and start talking about something else, and I notice an older man and woman, arm in arm, looking over at us and whispering. The man keeps nudging the woman, and I'm guessing she's his wife. Finally, they both walk up to us.

"'Scuse me, brothers," the man says. "We just had to come over and meet the legend himself!"

I look around, expecting to see somebody famous, but both the man and his wife have their eyes locked on Frankie Bell!

"How y'all doing?" Frankie Bell says, shaking both their hands.

"We flyin' high now!" the man says. "Spotted you from over there and said to my wife, 'Baby, I think that's Frankie Bell!' Didn't I tell you, Lucille?" he says triumphantly, like maybe they had a bet or something.

"Yeah, you called it, all right," the lady says.

"We got tickets to your Detroit and Cleveland shows," the man says, grinning big. "We'll be celebrating our fifty-fifth wedding anniversary with the Bell-Aires that weekend!"

"That so?" Frankie Bell asks. "I sho' appreciate the love! If y'all tell me your names, I'll make sure your seats are upgraded to the best in the house."

"Oh my Lord!" The lady presses a hand to her mouth. "I just can't believe this!"

"Curtis and Lucille Lainey," the man says. "Thank you so much, Mr. Bell, you've made our whole day!"

"Not as much as y'all made mine!" Frankie Bell tells them. "Moonie, take a picture of me and these beautiful people."

The Laineys really don't know how to work their phone, but I help them get to the camera and snap some pictures of them and Frankie Bell. They thank him again before walking off in disbelief that they just saw *the* Frankie Bell.

"Lawd, I guess yo' head ain't even gonna be able to

fit inside the stadium, now, is it?" Clyde says, shaking his head.

"How much you pay them to do that?" Monroe teases. I can tell they're real proud of him, though. I am, too.

I stare at my uncle and wonder for the first time who he really is, and how he got to be so good at what he does. I feel like I gotta hurry up and figure things out so I can be the exact same way.

CHAPTER 16

"You a lot like your grandfather . . .
always watching and thinking."

So much for starting a gaming club.

When I tell Adam what Mrs. Miller told me this morning—that we'll have to fill out a form, find an advisor, speak with the principal, write club goals, yada yada yada—he quickly loses interest.

"Nah, I'm good on all that," he says. "Plus, I gotta get ready for basketball. You sure you don't wanna try out? Coach Leo's been doing open gym after school."

And make a fool of myself? No thanks. I tell Adam no worries, but yo, I'm low-key worried. Latrell's got his thing, Adam's got his thing, and I've got . . . speech class.

Mr. G's a few minutes late to our session, but he's his usual happy self when he comes through the door.

"Xavier, killer socks, dude!" Mr. G says, pointing at my ABC socks.

Both Jared and Daysha look down at my feet.

"Thanks," I tell him. In his latest package to me, Frankie Bell wrote that he wasn't sure if I would embarrass the *blank* outta him while we were at Central, but since I didn't, I must be learning. Hence, alphabet socks.

"How many socks you got, anyway?" Daysha asks. I shrug. My collection's definitely growing, and so is the attention. I can't count how many times kids say, "Hey, Sock Boy!" when they see me now.

"M-maybe like t-t-twenty p-pairs," I say. I'm about to ask Mr. G how many bow ties he has, but Jared beats me to it, tapping his pencil the whole time.

"How many, how many bow ties do you have, Mr. G?"

Mr. G whistles and scratches his head.

"I honestly haven't counted in a while," he says. "I'll let you know at our next session, all right?"

"Yeah, that's cool, that's cool," Jared says.

Mr. G sets a timer and has us go through some phonics flash cards. It's super embarrassing to be sounding out words like "taxi" and "snowflake," but I don't stutter as much when I slow down. Mr. G's been teaching me this technique called cancellation, which basically means whenever I start stuttering I'm supposed to stop, relax, and really stretch the word out when I say it again. I feel a little dumb when I do it, but it's been helping.

"So, we're gonna do some group work today," Mr. G

says, which is kinda funny since we do group work *every* time. He holds up a glass jar that's filled with Popsicle sticks and starts shaking it around.

"I, and my dear sister, of course, stayed up pretty late one night eating popcorn and working on these scenarios for you guys."

Daysha coughs "No life!" into her hand, and I smile. Jared doesn't get it, and Mr. G forges ahead like he doesn't hear her.

"You each get to pick a Popsicle stick, and then you work together to act out or explain whatever scenario is written on your stick." Mr. G tips the jar to each of us and we reach in and grab a Popsicle stick. There's, like, hundreds inside, each with blue writing on it. Mine says, Your best friend is cheating on a test.

"Take about ten minutes, guys, and remember to practice the techniques we've been working on," Mr. G says. "Cancellation for Jared and Xavier, and Daysha, remember to take your time sounding things out."

Mr. G gets up and walks over to his other desk, and none of us makes a move to do anything.

"Hey, okay, which one should we do first?" asks Jared finally. "Mine says, 'You are sick on the day of basketball tryouts.'"

I use cancellation as I read through mine, then me and Jared look at Daysha.

"What?" she asks.

"What does yours say?" Jared asks.

Daysha sucks her teeth and holds the Popsicle stick toward us so we can read it. Daysha doesn't stutter like me, or repeat certain words and tap a pencil all over the place like Jared, but she can't read so good. I'm not sure if she even knows her Popsicle stick says, You have $20 to buy groceries for a birthday dinner.

We start acting out the three scenarios, and Mr. G's over there cracking up!

"I'm thinking I see three people who should be on their way to Broadway," he says. He makes a big deal of clapping and cheering like we just won an Oscar or something.

"I'm serious, lady and gentlemen. I'm seeing a lot of good progress," Mr. G tells us. "Keep it up!"

I'm feeling pretty good about what Mr. G said, but when I glance over at Daysha, she's rolling her eyes as usual. I don't know why this bothers me so much, but I decide to call her out when we're in sewing class.

"S-so h-how come y-you don't like Mr. G?" I ask.

"He's corny," she says, scrunching her face up.

I lower my voice. "But you l-l-like Mrs. Clark?" I ask.

"Mrs. Clark is amazing," Daysha says, looking at me like, *Duh!*

Since the bell hasn't rung yet and me and Daysha are

having this great conversation, I decide to go with another question.

"Why y-y-you in s-s-s ssspeeeech anyway? Y-y-yyyou don't st-st-sssstutter."

"Neither does Jared," Daysha says, avoiding the question.

I shrug. Jared might not stutter, but he definitely repeats words nonstop. Daysha doesn't do either of those things.

"I m-mean, it's c-cool," I say. "Y-you don't gotta t-t-tell m-me."

"I have dyslexia," Daysha says. I've heard that word before, but I'm not sure what it means exactly.

"S-s-so is M-Mr. G helping?" I ask.

"I mean, I guess," Daysha says with a shrug. "He just be doing the most sometimes."

I'm about to say he's not so bad, but Daysha turns the tables on me.

"So why are you in sewing?" she asks.

"I'm jjjuuuussssst exppppaaannding m-my horizons," I tell her with a grin, deciding to skip the whole scheduling story.

"Mmm-hmm," she says, a smirk on her face.

It feels good to know that she's over here *noticing* me. Now that I think about it, Daysha's kinda cute. The red cornrows look real nice on her.

The bell stops our conversation, but I notice that when she scoots her chair up, she also moves it a little closer to me.

"All right, all heaven's eleven accounted for," Mrs. Clark says after she takes attendance. She's really into this "heaven's eleven" thing, and so are the girls.

"Today I want to dive a little deeper into your service project," Mrs. Clark says. "We talked about it on the first day, but I decided to make a few changes."

I don't remember hearing anything about a service project, but the question Mrs. Clark asks next makes a light bulb go off in my head.

"Anyone want to be group leader on the service project?"

I hear the word "leader" and my hand shoots up before anyone else's. This is perfect! I can knock out leadership and service all at once!

"Okay, Xavier, thanks for volunteering," Mrs. Clark says.

"N-n-no p-problem," I say. I take a deep breath, use cancellation, and keep going. "Wh-what about a t-t-tttttoy drive?"

Christmas is less than two months away, and I'm sure the news would come and take pictures of us giving toys to little kids.

"Ummm, everybody does that," Tori says.

"Yeah, that's kinda basic," Alyssa adds. "This is sewing class, so we should, like, do something related to that. Just sayin'."

A few other girls agree, but nobody throws out any other ideas.

"It's not a bad idea, Xavier," Mrs. Clark says, "but your classmates do have some good points. So for homework, each of you needs to come up with a couple ideas for a service project. We'll discuss them on Monday, and you can decide on the one you like most."

I shake my head. I see what's going on here. I'm waaaay outnumbered, and we'll probably end up doing whatever they all want to do.

Not unless you wearin' the big drawls!

Frankie Bell's voice is in my head, and his voice is right. *I'm* the leader of this service project! So I gotta come up with an idea that they'll absolutely love.

And for that, I'm gonna need some backup.

CHAPTER 17

"I'm takin' you to see the future."

"**A**ll this cookin' I do round here, and you give the apron to this little girl?"

Aunt Kat got her hand on her hip and she's definitely not going "Awwww, how sweet!" when I hand Shannon the apron I made in sewing class.

"Oh. Ummm . . ." My mind races cuz Aunt Kat is legit upset. "That w-was just the p-practice one. You know I g-got one c-c-comin' for you, Aunt K-Kat." I wink when I say this and pat her arm.

"Mmm-hmm," she says. "You betta!"

"Can't believe you made this," Shannon says. She puts the apron on right away and starts snapping selfies on her cell phone. Her fingers tap the screen for a few seconds, then she looks up and grins.

"Posted on all my accounts!"

I suck my teeth. She's like Renee from the bus!

"C'mon, Shan!" I say. I'm not really trying to have it out there that I make . . . aprons.

"What? You betta use that!" Shannon says. "You never know."

I pretty much doubt apron-making is gonna help me out anytime soon, but I don't have time to worry about it with Shannon. I got something else I need from her.

"Hey, c-can I g-get Ju's number?" I ask casually. She raises an eyebrow.

"For what?"

"I need to t-talk to him," I say.

"About *what?*" Shannon asks. Man, she's so dang nosy!

"I g-got some questions for him," I tell her. "*Girl* questions."

"Are you serious right now?" Shannon says.

"What?"

"You wanna ask a *dude* a girl question, instead of a girl?"

I don't say anything. I guess she kinda has a point. So I tell her about my sewing class predicament.

"It's like b-being home," I tell her. "Always outnumbered!"

"It's not that hard, Xav," Shannon tells me. "All you

gotta do is come up with an idea that they can't resist. And don't make it about you."

"Okay, c-cool," I say. "So c-can I get J-Ju's number?"

"Wow." Shannon shakes her head.

"What?" I say. "You said what a g-girl would s-say, and I wanna hear what a guy would say."

"Do you, though?" Shannon asks.

"Yes!" Why she being so hard-core about it?

"Well, sometimes you just gotta figure stuff out on your own."

Shannon puts on the apron and goes to help Aunt Kat make dinner.

Why is everybody sounding more and more like Frankie Bell every day? I drag myself to the couch and turn on the TV. Even that doesn't last long, cuz a little while later Aunt Kat plops in her chair and tells me to turn to the six o'clock news.

See? Outnumbered everywhere.

I'm about to head up to my room to brainstorm ideas when Chris Carouthers, the Channel 19 news guy, says something that makes me freeze.

"With the weather growing cooler, one thing remains a hot commodity: socks!"

The camera pans over to the building Chris is standing in front of.

"I'm here with Joanne Jackson, director of the St. James Street House of Hope, and she says that while she can always count on amazing proceeds from their annual toy drive, some simpler needs of the house often go unmet. Joanne, can you tell us more about that?"

The Joanne lady says that sometimes guests at the house run out of basic things like toiletries and socks, and that she would love to see greater donations of those items, especially around the holidays.

"So as you donate those toys, don't forget to add the wool, too!" says Chris.

The camera moves over to Chris, and down to his feet, where he lifts his pant leg to show off his navy blue socks with a green-and-yellow paisley design.

"Like I say, the swag is in the socks! Back to you, Amanda!"

Aunt Kat says something about Amanda's wig not being right, but my mind is already connecting all the dots I needed. I know exactly what project idea will win the girls over, and sorry, Shannon, but it's gonna be about me.

CHAPTER 18

"You ain't no little baby anymore."

I walk into sewing class swagged out from head to toe, and I can feel the girls' eyes shift over to me.

"Whoa! You cut your hair," Alyssa says, staring at my head.

"Nope," I say, sliding into my seat. "B-but my b-b-bbbbarber did."

"You look different," Tori says.

"But nice," Daysha adds. "I mean, your hair looks nice."

I smirk. *Don't fight it, Daysha.*

But she's right; my hair finally looks nice. After a boatload of begging, Aunt Kat agreed to take me to get my hair cut by the barber Frankie Bell recommended. Aunt Kat grumbled, but the drive wasn't even that long!

Gone is the curly mess that had me looking like Sid the Science Kid. Shannon made me keep the curls on top, though, so what I'm rockin' now is a high-top fade with a lightning bolt on the side. And of course, I had to wear the lightning bolt socks to match. My ears do stick out a little bit, but overall, I'm feelin' good.

Mrs. Clark takes attendance, and when she asks what ideas we have for our service project, my hand's the first one in the air.

"Go ahead, Xavier, what did you come up with?" she asks.

"S-something th-that's u-usually overlooked," I say with a grin. "Socks."

"Socks?" Mrs. Clark raises an eyebrow and I hear Daysha go "OMG" under her breath.

"Y-yeah," I say, "m-most people w-w-wwwwwannnna do toy drives or c-coat drives, but places l-l-like House of Hope n-n-need s-socks. S-saw it on the n-n-nnnnews."

"Hmmm, interesting idea," Mrs. Clark says. She's not as blown away as I thought she'd be. "Anything else?"

I frown and shake my head. Yo, the sock idea is good enough!

Mrs. Clark writes "Sock Drive" on the board and goes to the next person.

"Well, I was gonna say a coat drive, but now . . ." Tori

looks over at me. I shrug. I can't help it if I'm the only one who thinks outside the box.

"We can go read to the kindergarten kids," Alyssa says.

"We can make aprons and sell them," Daysha says. "And we can donate the money to a homeless shelter or something."

"We can pick up trash around the library," says Carlita. Everybody shoots that down real quick.

At the end of it all, the board is filled and Mrs. Clark has us narrow things down to our top three ideas.

"Honestly, I like Xavier's idea," says Shyanne. "Especially since he's into socks and everything. Where do you be getting your socks anyway?"

"Classified," I tell her. Which, of course, is gonna make her wanna know even more.

The girls also decide to keep the reading-to-kids idea and the idea about having a dance to raise awareness about something. They don't know what exactly to raise awareness about, but I can tell they really just wanna have a dance.

So I use that.

"How 'b-bout this," I say. "We do the d-d-dance, and to g-get in, you have to donate s-socks. Then w-w-we give the socks to that p-place from the news."

There's a moment of silence while the ladies ponder my idea.

"Well, that's a creative twist," Mrs. Clark says.

I see a few nods around the room.

"It's cool, I guess," Alyssa says.

"What kind of socks?" Tori asks.

"R-regular ones." I shrug, then stick out my foot. "Or s-s-swaggy ones."

The girls start talking about the dance and how many pairs of socks we should "charge" for admission. They're getting into it—right where I want them to be. It's super satisfying to watch Mrs. Clark erase the other ideas off the board and circle mine.

"We need a name for the dance," Shyanne says, and we all start brainstorming.

"Sock Hop?"

"Girl, nah!"

"Socked-Up Dance?"

"Ugh, no!"

"How 'bout the Sock 'n Sole Dance? Like, shoe soles?"

When Carlita says that, we all stop and think.

"I like it." Tori nods. "Sock 'n Sole is kinda cool. It can be a no-shoes-allowed dance; we all wear socks instead."

Everyone likes that idea, so I decide now's the time to hit 'em with all I got. I spent hours playing the ceiling game and brainstorming to come up with this. . . .

"Brought t-to you b-by . . ." I take a deep breath. "The Sole Crew."

"You really doin' the most right now," Alyssa says.

"What? W-we should have a group n-name," I say. "We care, *and* s-socks are important, r-right, Mrs. Clark?"

"I did share the importance of socks, yes," Mrs. Clark admits.

"But do we really need a class name?" Tori asks.

The truth is, she's right; we don't *have* to have a class name. But I can picture Chris Carouthers standing in front of that same building, and it's gonna sound so good when he announces the largest sock donation in history, given by the Sole Crew. And of course, his interview of the Sole Crew leader, Xavier Moon, is gonna be even more amazing.

"I'm cool with it," Shyanne says. "Maybe we can do more than one Sock 'n Sole Dance."

Yes! Shyanne is really coming in clutch!

Even though Mrs. Clark moves on to our assignment for the day, you can write it in the history books: today marks the birth of the Sole Crew.

When the bell rings, Mrs. Clark stops me at the door and says, "Really good work today, Mr. Moon."

"Thanks," I tell her with a grin. Sole Crew leader today, Scepter League man tomorrow!

CHAPTER 19

"Moonie, the time is now."

"Hey, it's our reigning Sock King," Mrs. Miller says when I walk into the main office. "Let's see what you got today!"

Since it's too cold for shorts now, I've been wearing a lot of joggers so my socks can still be on display. Shannon clowns me for having the pant legs pulled up a tiny bit more than the average person, but it gets the job done. We're not even to Thanksgiving break yet, and already I'm known for my socks.

I stretch out my foot and Mrs. Miller leans over the desk to check out my socks, which are dark blue with different-colored clocks all over them. Frankie Bell's note with them was short: *Moonie, the time is now. Stop waiting.*

Is it just me, or is Frankie Bell psychic or something?

It's like he knows I got something big to do today and is giving me a pep talk. Me, Alyssa, and Tori are meeting with Principal Roland to get his approval for the Sock 'n Sole Dance, and even though the girls are great at talking, I know I gotta take the lead. There's no way Frankie Bell could know about the dance and the Sole Crew, so how is he doing this? It's low-key scary.

"You are making quite the statement this year, Xavier," Mrs. Miller says. "What can I help you with?"

"We h-h . . . hhhhave a m-m-m . . . mmmmeeting with the p-principal," I say, showing her the pass Mrs. Clark wrote us.

"You're just a little early, so have a seat, and he'll be ready for you soon," Mrs. Miller says.

I smirk as I sit down, Frankie Bell's words in my head. *To be early is to be on time. . . .*

While I wait for Alyssa and Tori to show up, I go over what I'm gonna say in my head and remind myself that I need to take deep breaths, shake Mr. Roland's hand, and look him in the eyes while I'm talking. I've never actually talked with him before, just nodded or moved out his way in the halls, cuz he's kinda intense.

Alyssa and Tori come in the office—laughing and talking, as usual—and plop down in the chairs next to me.

"You didn't go to lunch?" Tori asks.

"Nah," I say, ignoring the tiny rumble in my stomach.

"I ate so fast I feel like I'm gonna throw up," Alyssa says. She opens her purse and pops a piece of gum in her mouth. Tori takes a piece, too, but I shake my head when she holds the pack out to me.

"Oh yeah, you can't chew gum with braces, right?" she asks.

I'm about to tell her I can do anything I want with braces (sort of), I just don't wanna be smacking gum while talking to the principal, when at that exact moment, Mr. Roland's door swings open and he appears.

Mr. Roland's a big dude, and most kids are scared of him, even if they'll never admit it. His locs are pulled back into a ponytail and hang below his shoulders. I wonder what I would look like with locs. My dad used to have them, and Aunt Kat would call him Black Jesus as a joke.

"You three here for me?" Mr. Roland asks.

"Yes, they're your twelve fifteen," Mrs. Miller tells him.

"Well, c'mon back," Mr. Roland says. We follow him to his office, and as soon as we're inside, I hold out my hand. Mr. Roland squeezes my hand super tight and smiles.

"Th-th . . . thhhhanks for t-t-t . . . ttttaking the time to m-m . . . mmmmeet with us," I say, hating the way

I sound right now, but knowing Mr. G would want me using cancellation everywhere, not just in our sessions.

"I should be thanking the three of you," he says. "You're giving up your lunchtime just to talk to me."

"Well, we ate lunch," Alyssa says, pointing to herself and Tori. "We just had to be super quick."

"Can't be mad at that," Mr. Roland laughs, and sits down behind his desk. "What can I help you with?"

"We're in Mrs. Clark's s-s- . . . sssssewing class and w-w-w . . . wwwwe want to have a d-d . . . dddance for our service p-p . . . ppproject."

"Mrs. Clark said we'd have to get permission from you," Tori adds.

"Explain to me how a dance would work as a service project?" Mr. Roland asks. He looks skeptical, so I get the feeling we really gotta sell him on this. I feel Tori and Alyssa eyeing me, so I take a deep breath and explain the need for socks in our area, how we'd collect socks for the dance and then donate them to the House of Hope. It takes a long time to get it all out, but I make sure I'm looking right at Mr. Roland and speaking with confidence even though I probably sound like a train wreck.

"I remember seeing that news report," Mr. Roland says when I'm finished. "I gotta say, this is a very creative idea; great job."

Alyssa, Tori, and I all look at each other and grin. A little too soon.

"I have a few questions for you, though," Mr. Roland continues, rubbing his chin. "Student council usually hosts a winter dance as a fundraiser. Having two dances in such a short period of time is probably not a good idea."

Dang! I didn't think about that at all. My mouth opens and my brain races to come up with a solution on the spot.

"My sister is the student council president," Alyssa says while I'm still thinking. "They're cool with having a bake sale during our dance instead."

This is definitely news to me. I try not to look shocked. How come she thought of that and I didn't?

"Sounds like a good compromise." Mr. Roland nods. He asks a few more questions, and mostly Alyssa and Tori answer.

"Oh, and our class will also make socks to donate," Tori says.

Huh? I don't remember that part at all! I try not to let my face give me away, but as the leader, I need to speak up.

"I can tell you young folks have done some good planning, and I like the unique twist on service," Mr. Roland says. He leans forward and nods at my socks. "Lemme guess; socks were your idea?"

"Y-yes, s-sir," I say quickly, sitting up straighter. "I'm the l-leader of the S-Sole Crew."

"Well, good work, all of you," Mr. Roland says. "I see no problem with you hosting a—what did y'all call it? A Sock 'n Sole Dance? I like that name."

"Thanks, Mr. Roland!" Alyssa says with a big grin.

We head out of his office just as the end-of-lunch bell rings. The girls are walking ahead of me, already talking about who they want to go to the dance with.

"Latrell be looking so goooood!" Alyssa says. "It's an instant yes if he asks me!"

"He betta ask you," says Tori. "Didn't you get him that wristband once he got in the League?"

"Yup! Cost me ten bucks, too!" Alyssa turns around so fast, I almost crash into her. "Xavier, when you tell your boy about the dance, make sure you hype me up, aight?"

"I g-g-got you," I tell her. But as I think about it, the Sole Crew leader should show up to the dance with somebody, too, right? Tori and Alyssa might as well return the favor. So I decide to shoot my shot for one of the cutest girls in the school.

"Y'all kn-know Shyanne's c-cousin, Renee?"

CHAPTER 20

*"I'ma say it again, if you don't get
yourself together this year, it might
never happen."*

It's real nice outside for early November, so after my Saturday call with Ma, Aunt Kat takes advantage of the weather by making me wash her car.

"All this means is that ol' man winter 'bout to kick the snot outta us in a few days!" she says, following me outside to read the paper on the porch while I work. She's right; it'll probably be a blizzard tomorrow.

I'm just about done scrubbing the gunk off Aunt Kat's windshield when a voice calls out, "Perfect day for a car wash, ain't it?"

I look over my shoulder and see Mr. Talbert walking toward us.

"Looks like you doin' a fine job here, Xavier Moon," he tells me. "I had a car, I'd be lined up to have you do mine next!"

"Th-thanks," I say. "You d-don't have a c-c-c . . . ccccar?"

"Naw, I just let these here legs take me where I need to go," he says. "How you doin', Miz Katherine?"

"I'm just fine, Luke, and you? Looks like you going on a walk this beautiful afternoon?"

"No, ma'am, I done got that out the way. Got some Parker House rolls on my mind, so I figure I better go make some!"

"Well, don't be shy 'bout sending some our way!" Aunt Kat says.

"You know I will!" Mr. Talbert laughs. "Y'all take care now."

"B-bye," I say.

"Y'all kids probably think that man's a little different, but he got reason to be," Aunt Kat says, watching Mr. Talbert climb his front porch and go inside. I stop scrubbing and look over at Aunt Kat. Sounds like a story's coming.

"What y'all don't know is that he lost his daughter years ago, way before you were even thought of," Aunt Kat says. "She was hit by a bus. Just a terrible, terrible thing. Shook him up real bad. I suppose that's why he's out there every morning, makin' sure kids get on the bus safely."

Wow. Of course I didn't know any of that, and I guess it makes sense about him always being at our bus stop.

"Are h-him and Frankie B-Bell f-friends?" I ask.

"Yeah, I'd say they were. Hit it off from the start, when we moved onto this street," Aunt Kat says. "But Frankie Bell was always into music, so whenever the road called, he answered. Luke, on the other hand, never lived no-where but here on Larmity."

I turn on the hose and rinse off Aunt Kat's car and think about what kind of guy I'll be: the kind like Frankie Bell, who travels around and sees everything, or the kind like Mr. Talbert, who sees everything there is to see in one spot. Maybe I'll be some of both: check stuff out from my window, but also leave the room to do things up close.

For some reason, I always liked watching the sudsy water run down the driveway and then down the street to the right. Kinda cool to think we must be up a tiny bit higher than the houses on that side. The way I notice stuff like that, I'm thinking I'll probably be a guy more like Mr. Talbert.

When I'm done with the car, Aunt Kat reaches in her bra and hands me a warm twenty-dollar bill. I try not to make a face as I take it with two fingers. Aunt Kat cackles.

"It ain't gonna bite you, boy!" she says. "And trust me, it'll spend the same."

"Thanks," I tell her, pushing the money into my pocket.

"Oh Lord, here comes trouble," Aunt Kat grumbles, looking down the street. I turn and see Ju walking toward us. This is actually perfect; I could use some tips on how to ask Renee to the Sock 'n Sole Dance. She sits by me almost every day on the bus, always snapping a pic of my socks. But should I ask her on the bus, with everybody all around? Ju gotta help me out!

"Hey, Miz Kat; how you doin'?" Ju says, turning on his megawatt smile.

"Hmmph!" Aunt Kat pokes her lips out a mile. "I am just fine. Question is, how are *you*?"

"I'm good," Ju says. "Busy with school and stuff."

"Mmm-hmm, where's that car of yours?" asks Aunt Kat.

"At home." Ju shrugs. "I thought me and Shannon could go on a walk, since it's nice out."

"A walk, huh?" Aunt Kat stands.

"Yes, ma'am," Ju says with a smile. Sometimes I think he likes the way Aunt Kat hates on him. He's so sure he's gonna win her over no matter what.

"Wait out here; I'll see if she wanna go anywhere on foot," Aunt Kat says, going into the house.

"Wassup, Xav," Ju says, nodding toward me.

"Hey," I say. "You know she's m-m-mad at you."

"Who, Miz Kat? She's always mad," Ju laughs.

"N-nah, man." I shake my head. "Sh-Shannon."

Shannon's cooking club had a cooking demo yesterday, and she came home from that with a major attitude. Turns out Ju was supposed to be there but stood her up. At least that's what I figured out from snooping by her door when she was on the phone with one of her friends.

"You talkin' 'bout the cooking thing?" Ju asks. "We're past that, dawg."

I give him a look like I don't believe him. "So l-last night she was p-p-pissed, and t-today she's good?"

"Exactly," Ju says, pointing at me like I finally got it. "I had a League meeting that came up, so I couldn't make it to her thing. But today, we gonna go on this walk, get a little snack or whatever, and then we're gonna watch that cooking show she likes."

Ju comes up the porch steps and sits in the chair Aunt Kat was in.

"Cool," I say, sitting in the other chair and trying to look as cool as Ju.

"We havin' this d-d-dance at m-my school," I say after a few seconds.

"Yeah?" Ju's scrolling on his phone and doesn't even look up.

"Yeah, it was m-m-m . . . mmmmy idea."

"You goin' with somebody?" Ju asks, still glued to his cell.

"Yeah," I say. "I m-mean, hopefully."

Ju finally looks up. "You ask her yet?"

I shake my head and he starts grinning.

"Ohhh, okay, I get it. You need some advice from the master," he says.

"I mean, if y-you g-got some tips or s-s-something," I say.

"Yeah, I got a tip," Ju laughs. "Just ask her, bro! Tell her the dance gonna be lit, especially if y'all go together."

I don't know why I'm expecting something more, something bigger, especially coming from a Scepter Leaguer. I thought for sure Ju would say something like send her flowers, or get her favorite candy, or write her a dope poem. But just ask her? C'mon!

"You nervous to say something?" Ju asks, nudging my arm with his.

"N-nah," I say, making a face.

"Good. Stop playin' around and just do it," Ju tells me. "While you over here thinking about it, some other dude is out there just doing it. That's facts, dawg."

Shannon comes onto the porch right then, arms crossed in front of her and lips poked out.

"Hey, babe," Ju says, standing up and grinning. I shake my head. He's about to get shut down.

"I'm still mad at you, Ju," she says, glaring at him.

"No, you not," Ju says, pulling her into a hug. "And you definitely not gonna be after a double scoop of bubble gum ice cream and watching Mel Francis on *Chef's Up*."

"Next time you betta be there," Shannon tells him, still pouting.

"I will be," Ju says. "You ready to walk?"

"Yeah," Shannon says.

"Aight, X, catch ya later," Ju says as they head down the steps. "'Member what I told you."

"What did you tell him?" Shannon asks, sucking her teeth.

"Grown-man business; don't worry about it," Ju tells her.

"Xavier, don't be listening to him!" Shannon calls as Ju pulls her down the street.

I wave at my sister, but I'm not promising anything. In fact, tomorrow at school, I'm gonna do exactly what Ju said.

CHAPTER 21

"Take this seriously, Moonie."

When Mrs. Clark passes out our midterm grades in class today, I'm shocked to see an A staring at me and the words Excellent job, Xavier! right underneath.

For this to just be an elective class, that midterm was a beast! We had to label a diagram of a sewing machine, know about a bunch of different designers, and define some sewing terms. And then Mrs. Clark went left field on us. She brought in a bunch of clothes that needed repairs and we each had to pick one item to fix. I picked a black shirt that was ripped on both sides, and when I sewed it up, I used thick red thread. It ended up looking like a design instead of a fix-up, and I saw all the girls eyeing it when I turned it in.

"What'd you get?" Daysha asks. Her paper's all out in the open, so I see the B+ on it.

"Oh, I d-did aight," I say.

"What are you gonna do for the final project?"

I shrug, and Daysha launches into her idea for a jogging suit.

"I'm gonna have my own clothing line one day," she tells me. "It's gonna be called 'All Day.'"

"Cool," I say.

"Wowwwww," Daysha says after staring at me for a few seconds.

"What?"

"You're actually good at this, but you don't even care about it."

"I mean . . . it's s-s-s . . . ssssewing," I say. I don't know why she's making a big deal about it. Sewing's not my thing.

But then Mrs. Clark announces that as a class we did really well on the midterm, and that there were only two A's in our class. I know I have one of them, and that makes me think . . . *is* sewing my thing?

The Sole Crew (minus Daysha, who has basketball tryouts) had made plans to stay after school and decorate posters for the dance, so we all walk to the art room when the last bell rings. When Mr. Lopez, the art teacher I *should've* had, goes to get extra poster boards from the teachers' supply room, Shyanne clears her throat loudly.

"Okay, let's just get something out the way," she says, folding her arms across her chest. "Who got the other A?"

The girls all look around the room, and it's Carlita who speaks up.

"I bet it was Xavier."

"I knew it!" Tori says.

"Yeah, his remixed shirt was kinda fire," says Alyssa. A few other girls nod and agree.

Wait, what? Other than the fact that they're talking about me like I'm not in the room, I'm surprised most of them guessed that I got an A.

"I think your shirt stood out more, and Mrs. Clark likes that kind of stuff," Tori says.

"And you must've did real good on the written part," Shyanne says.

Not gonna lie, I studied pretty hard for this midterm, mostly because I don't want Mrs. Clark to change her mind about me being our class leader. And yeah, I been spending a lot of time watching people design stuff on YouTube, but that's mainly for class. Mrs. Clark had assigned us this video about Daymond John, a guy who started a clothing company called FUBU, and after that, I started watching all these other design videos. Maybe I'll be like Daysha and have my own company one day, too.

"So we got everything covered?" Tori asks once we're finished making the posters.

"Yup," I say, and nod. "Sh-Shyanne m-m . . . mmm-makes the announcement in the m-m-m . . . mmmmorn-ing, y-you bring in donation b-b- . . . bbbbins for the s-socks, and we got the d-d-deejay and decorations on lock."

Carlita's cousin is Jump22, a popular deejay in the city, and he agreed to do our dance, as long as he could get all the "corny middle school dance food" for free. His girlfriend always decorates for his events, so she's gonna help out in that department. Everything about this came together really good, and what Tori says next makes it even better.

"Oh, forgot to tell you guys, someone from *CitySpeak* will be there to cover the fundraiser," Tori tells us.

Everybody gets hyped about that, and I do, too. *City-Speak* newspapers are always *everywhere:* grocery stores, barbershops, restaurants, movie theaters. What I don't tell Sole Crew is that *I've* been working on something even bigger . . . reaching out to Chris Carouthers from Channel 19. If he comes to the Sock 'n Sole Dance and sees all the socks we collect, the Sole Crew is guaranteed to be all over the news *and* in the paper. Right in Mr. Donnel's face.

We each grab posters and spread out to hang them up around school. The first place I pick? The bulletin board outside the office, where the Scepter League poster used to be. It feels good to tape it up, see my idea hanging there. The Scepter League is supposed to be about service, but I don't see them doing nothing like *this*.

Once I'm finished there, I hang a poster outside the lunchroom, and on the gym door. I'm stepping back to admire my work when a whistle blows inside the gym, and a few seconds later, the door busts open and a group of girls come out, breathing heavy.

One of them is Daysha. I study her face, but she doesn't give anything away.

"H-how'd it g-g-go?"

"It was aight." She shrugs.

"Y-you feel g-good about it?"

"I'm ready," Daysha says, "so, yeah."

"Cool," I say. I don't bust her bubble by telling her that's exactly how I felt about the League.

"Y'all did good with the posters," Daysha says, checking out the one on the gym door. "I think the dance is gonna be lit!"

I don't know why, but I immediately think about what Ju told me to say, *The dance gonna be lit, especially if we go together!* I gotta make sure I ask Renee tomorrow.

According to Alyssa, there's a few eighth graders who like her, so I need to make a move fast!

"Hey, how you gettin' home?" Daysha asks, checking something on her phone.

"My aunt K-Kat," I say.

"Think I can get a ride? My mom texted that she completely forgot about my tryouts."

"Y-yeah, of c-course," I say. We walk to the doors and I get a little nervous when I see Aunt Kat's car screech to a stop. She doesn't like when people spring things on her, so I'm praying the whole walk to the car that she won't trip about this.

"Aunt Kat, c-c-can we give Daysha a r-ride home?" I ask when I open the door. "She lives on the b-b-block."

Aunt Kat peers at Daysha before waving her into the car. *Thank God!*

"So you was makin' posters for the dance, too?" Aunt Kat asks, looking at Daysha in the rearview mirror as she pulls out of the drive.

"Well, I woulda been, but I had basketball tryouts," Daysha says.

"Oh, you that lil' girl who's always at the park practicin'!" Aunt Kat says, turning around to look closer at Daysha and swerving a little.

"Aunt K-Kat!" I say, pointing at the road. Man, Shannon better get a license quick!

"I see what I'm doing, boy!" Aunt Kat grumbles as she straightens the wheel. "I was just about to tell the young lady that all that practicin' gonna pay off. I used to be somethin' else on the court back in the day, ya know."

"WHAT?" I say it louder than I mean to, and I probably shouldn't be laughing, cuz Aunt Kat swats my arm. "Owww!"

"Stop acting like you shocked! I was good!"

"I b-believe you!" I tell Aunt Kat, trying not to grin. Then I shut up and let the two of them talk basketball all the way home. Who knew?

When we turn onto Larmity and get close to Walter's house, he comes bounding outside and chases the car.

"You guys went on a date without me?" Walter asks, looking half-hurt, half-mischievous.

"We were at school, Walter," Daysha says.

"Your school was over two hours ago," Walter points out. Then he notices Daysha's gym bag, and the fact that she's still wearing basketball shorts.

"Ohhhh, it was the tryouts!" he squeaks, jumping up and down and grabbing Daysha's arm. "Did you make the team?"

"Chill, dude," Daysha says. "I won't know till Friday."

"That's a lie!" Aunt Kat calls from the car. "She already knows right now!"

Daysha can't hide her grin at that.

"Thanks for the ride," she tells Aunt Kat. "Bye, Xavier."

"Bye," I say.

Aunt Kat backs out of Daysha's driveway and turns the car around abruptly, almost taking out the fire hydrant in front of the Johnsons' house.

"Hummmph," Aunt Kat says, glaring at me. "You over there grinning, Moonie, but I could teach you a thing or two!"

I just smile and shake my head. She probably could.

CHAPTER 22

"See ya up the mountain, Moonie."

" **I** still can't believe my baby bro has a date!"

Shannon's helping me with my tie and she's said this a million times already. The truth is, I can't believe it either . . . at all. The day after the posters went up, Renee sat next to me on the bus again and snapped pictures of my socks for her daily IG post. I thought about what Ju said and played it real cool, told her that if she liked these socks, she should see the ones I'm wearing to the dance . . . up close and personal.

"You askin' me to the dance?" Renee had said with a smirk on her face. Almost made me lose my nerve!

"D-does it s-sound like I am?"

"Ummm, yes," she said.

"Then, yeah," I said. "I'm askin' you t-t . . . ttttto my dance."

"Aight, bet," Renee said. "We gotta donate five pairs of socks to get in, right?"

And just like that, I had a date to the Sock 'n Sole Dance.

"There, got it!" Shannon says, tugging on my tie for the last time. Mr. G gave me a real bow tie to wear to the dance, and after thirty minutes of YouTubing, we (mostly Shannon) finally figured out how to tie it.

"Thanks, Shan," I say, checking myself out in the mirror.

The tie is a gray, black, and green paisley, and Shannon helped me pick out a white shirt with dark green stripes. The thing that sets it off, though? Suspenders. Dark green ones. Never thought I'd ever wear these in my life, but Shannon basically forced me to.

"I guarantee you, won't be nobody else wearing suspenders there," Shannon says, like she can read my mind. "Awwww, look at my baby!"

"Okay, now for the socks and shoes. You're not wearing those, are you?" Shannon glances at my feet. I'm wearing plain white socks right now; Frankie Bell's orders. I got a package in the mail yesterday and his note said,

Moonie, don't open the package until the day of the dance, and don't put on what's inside until you are at

the dance. Am I clear? I think you know by now that
I'll find out if you decide to be hardheaded. Trust me.
—Frankie Bell

I don't know why he gotta be so cryptic all the time, or why I actually do what he says. But it's worked so far, and that's probably why I put the package of unopened socks into my bookbag with other stuff I'll need for the dance: deodorant, Tic Tacs, Carmex, cocoa butter.

"Ju's here; you ready?" Shannon asks me, tapping on her phone.

Deep breath. *I was born ready!*

"Yeah."

It took a lot of begging, but Aunt Kat's letting Shannon and Ju drop me and Daysha at school before the dance. Since we're Sole Crew, we gotta get there early and set up. I wish I was riding with Renee, but I have to settle for meeting up with her later.

It's legit cold outside, and little flakes are drifting around here and there. The back of my head is freezing, but there's no way I'm messing up my hair with a hat. I pull the hood of my coat up around my ears and race to Ju's car.

"So your girl lives down the street?" Ju asks once we're inside.

"Huh?" I ask, before realizing he's talking about

Daysha. "Sh-ssshe's n-n-nnnot my girl. M-my date is an eighth grader."

Ju obviously doesn't get that this is a big deal. At Rosewood, eighth graders stick together for everything. But not tonight!

"Oh, okay, dawg, my bad!" Ju laughs. "You never know."

When Daysha climbs into the back seat, I'm low-key shocked that her red cornrows are gone! Instead, she's got a giant Afro puff that looks nice on her. She's got on dancing-feet earrings, too.

"Hey, girl, those boots are cute!" Shannon says.

"Thanks," says Daysha with a grin. "And thanks for the ride."

"You got it," says Ju. "I trust y'all will behave yourselves at this dance, right?"

I groan and Shannon punches Ju on the shoulder.

"Owww! What?" he says. Shannon gives him a look and turns on the radio, which makes things less awkward.

"Wait, lemme see your bow tie," Daysha says, leaning toward me. I open my coat at the top and she points at her legs and goes, "No way!"

I look down at her leggings, and I swear, Sole Crew didn't talk about what we were wearing or anything, but her leggings look a lot like my tie! She takes off a boot and shows me her socks, which are white with green polka dots. Pretty cool.

"Great m-m-mmmminds," I tell her. Tonight, I'm trying another strategy that Mr. G taught us, where I don't pause when I'm stuttering, but I still stretch out my words. It's called a pull-out, and Mr. G says to get on the sound and not be afraid of the stutter.

We spend the rest of the ride bobbing our heads to the music, sometimes rapping along to what's playing. I catch Ju's eyes in the mirror once, and he gives that "do your thing, lil' man" grin.

We get to the school early, but Carlita's cousin, Jump22, already has the gym looking amazing! He's setting up his deejay equipment, and I can already tell the sound is gonna be great. Mr. G is here, too. Him and some lady I haven't seen before are helping with the decorating. We take our shoes off near the door, where there's an area roped off and a sign that says KICKS KORNER.

"Xavier! Good to see you, man!" Mr. G comes over and holds his fist out. "Nice tie!"

Mr. G sees Daysha and does this exaggerated bow that makes her laugh instead of roll her eyes.

"Hello, Lady Daysha! I am loving those earrings!"

"Hey, Mr. G," Daysha says. "You so corny!"

"Well, what do you guys think?" Mr. G asks, gesturing around the room.

"It's tight," Daysha tells him.

"Litty lit, right?" Mr. G says.

"Ummm, don't ever say that again, okay?" says the lady who's with Mr. G. She holds out her hand and says, "Hi there, I'm Allison. I see my brother has indoctrinated you with bow ties, huh?"

"Hi," I say, shaking her hand.

"This is Daysha, and this good man here is Xavier, and trust me, he's got his own thing," Mr. G says. "Wait till you see his socks, Allie."

They both look down, expecting to see magic.

"Oh, I haven't p-p-ppput them on y-y-yyyet," I say.

"Ahhh, I see," Mr. G says, winking. "Your socks are gonna make a grand entrance."

The truth is, I have no clue what my socks are gonna do. *Frankie Bell, don't let me down!*

"Well, I can't wait to see them," Allison says. "Nice to meet you, Xavier and Daysha."

"N-n-nnnice m-m-mmmeeting you, too," I tell her.

"We're hanging some lights over on this wall if you wanna lend a hand," Mr. G says.

As we walk over to where Mrs. Clark and Shyanne are, Mr. G leans closer and lowers his voice. "I gotta say, you're doing great with the pull-out." It feels good to know all this speech work is paying off.

The first thing I notice about Shyanne are her socks. She's got her shoes off and her socks go all the way up to her knees and have purple and silver swirls. They're pretty hypnotizing.

"Hey, Xavier," Shyanne says. Like everyone else, she stares at my feet. "Ummm, where's your socks?"

"Yeah," says Daysha. "You supposed to be the Sock King?"

"J-just wait," I tell them. The anticipation is definitely building, and I hope it's worth it.

I emailed Chris Carouthers from Channel 19 three times, from my school email and my personal one. I even mailed one of our flyers to the news station and said we wanted to donate all the socks we get to House of Hope. Haven't heard a thing from him. If Tori's *CitySpeak* connection doesn't show up, my whole plan falls apart.

"You aight?" Daysha asks me after we finish with the decorations.

"Yeah," I say.

"You don't seem like it," she tells me. "You gonna change socks?"

It's ten minutes to six, and Jump22 is starting to play music. A few kids are here already, handing their sock donation to Shyanne and checking in their shoes with Mr. G. Guess it's time to see what Frankie Bell sent me.

"I'll b-be right back," I tell Daysha. I go over to the section of shoes and pull off my bookbag. I open the package and see a second note taped inside.

Moonie,
You are the swag now.
—Frankie Bell

When I see what the note is attached to, my heart drops all the way to my white socks. What I'm holding in my hands is a pair of plain black socks.

I cannot believe Frankie Bell did this to me! The *most* important day for me to wear socks, and he sends me the most basic pair ever! And these cryptic messages are getting old; he needs to just say what he's trying to say. I'm at a sock-themed dance with plain socks. How is that swag?

I put on the socks, only because they look better than the white ones. I ask Mr. G if he can watch my bookbag, and for a split second I almost volunteer to take his job watching the shoes. Renee's gonna show up ready to see what I'm rockin' on my feet, and I'm gonna look like an idiot. Thanks a lot, Frankie Bell.

"Where's your boy Latrell?" Alyssa asks. The two of them are supposed to be talking now, and she's been looking around for him since she got here. Truth is, me and him haven't hung out a lot recently. He's been busy with the League, and I been busy with Sole Crew and this dance.

"Who knows," I tell Alyssa.

"Those the socks you're wearing?" Alyssa asks. She's got on socks covered with cups of hot cocoa, and I get mad all over again.

"Yeah, Alyssa, wh-what it l-l-llllook like?" I snap.

"I'm just sayin'." Alyssa shrugs. "I thought *you* of all people would come with amazing socks. Did you see Shyanne's?"

"Nah," I say. I know I'm being a little rude, and I'm lying, but I'm not looking forward to hearing these same questions all night. *I'm* the Sock King, and I'm out here looking mad basic.

"Oooh, there he is; see ya!" Alyssa says, taking off toward the gym door.

It's been mostly sixth graders coming in at first, but I look over just in time to see the Scepter Leaguers making their entrance. They all have on their jackets, of course, along with black pants, white shirts, and the green-and-gold League tie.

"Wassup, Xavier?" Latrell says when he comes over to add his shoes to the pile. Green-and-gold socks. I should probably disappear right now.

"Hey," I say, giving him a nod.

"Yo, I heard you got that girl Renee to be your date; where she at?"

That's a good question. Renee said she was getting here a little after six, but I don't see her. I'm not trying to be all desperate and ask Shyanne, either.

"N-n-not here y-yet," I say.

"Oh, that's wassup, probably coming in late on purpose," Latrell says. He glances at my feet, but before he has a chance to ask about my socks, Principal Roland hops on the mic to welcome everyone to the dance and to remind us all that it's for a good cause.

"Shout out to the Sole Crew for showing us that service can also be fun. Enough talkin'; let's get our Sock 'n Sole on!"

Jump22 plays a song that gets everybody hyped, and Latrell wanders off to dance with Alyssa. I'm just standing around watching. Like old Xavier would.

"Why ain't you dancing?" Daysha yells over the music. I shrug. I didn't even notice her come over. To be honest, I'm not a bad dancer. Just not feelin' it right now. Daysha rolls her eyes and grabs my elbow.

"C'mon!" she says. She must've learned from Walter how to drag people around, because the next thing I know, we're in the middle of the gym and there's no way I can just stand there without looking dumb. The gym lights dim and the disco lights start splashing colors everywhere. Everybody goes crazy.

That's when a miracle happens.

Daysha yells, "WHOA!" and points at my socks. I look down, too.

My socks . . . are now glowing, with blasts of fireworks blinking in different spots every few seconds. My socks look like a fireworks show! FRANKIE BELL IS A FREAKIN' GENIUS!

"That's fiyah, Xavier!" Daysha says. Other kids around us notice, too, and some of them whip out their phones to take snaps of my socks.

"I see you," Daysha says. "Had us all fooled!"

I just grin. Shoot, *I* was fooled, too! These fireworks socks change the game. I loosen up, and me and Daysha dance until we're hot and thirsty. I'm having fun and not even thinking about Renee, who *still* hasn't shown up! In the middle of one of my favorite songs, I see something in the gym doorway that makes me squint and look closer. It's a shadow at first, but once I see the hat, I know.

It's Frankie Bell.

"Y-yo, h-h-hhhhold on," I tell Daysha, and race over to the door. Frankie Bell's laughing with Principal Roland, and when he sees me, his smile widens.

"There he is, man of the hour!" Frankie Bell drapes a heavy arm around my shoulders. "I see you, nephew!"

"Frankie B-B-Bell, y-y-you're h-h-here," I stammer, forgetting all my speech techniques.

"It appears that I am," Frankie Bell says with a chuckle. "Bet you didn't trust me 'bout them socks, didja?"

"I m-mean, they were p-ppplain black," I tell him.

"That's what you and everyone else thought," Frankie Bell says. "But once the lights dropped and you got to movin', what happened? You figured out you got the best socks in the room!"

"S-s-ssso you gonna c-come dance?" I ask.

Frankie Bell laughs and pulls a handkerchief from his pocket to wipe his forehead.

"Moonie, my bones too old to do all that," he says. "I just stopped through to see your lil' event. You done good, nephew."

"Th-thanks," I say. Then I scrunch up my face. "H-h-hold up; h-h-how'd you kn-know about the d-d-dance?" I know for sure I never mentioned it to him, so how did he know to send socks *and* show up?

"Too many questions, not enough time! Now, where's

that date of yours?" Frankie Bell asks. "Cain't leave before seeing her!"

"Sh-she's, um . . . ," I say, feeling mad embarrassed about the whole Renee situation. I'm just about to tell Frankie Bell some elaborate story (or the truth), when Daysha shows up and hands me a cup.

"Tori said the punch is selling out, so I got you one," she says. Frankie Bell looks from Daysha to me, and a grin inches across his face.

"Must be some mighty good punch, then," he says.

"I can get you some if you want," Daysha offers. Frankie Bell reaches into his wallet and pulls out a twenty-dollar bill.

"That would be marvelous, young lady," he says. "Please keep the change for your fundraiser."

Show-off.

"Well, don't just stand there staring at me!" Frankie Bell says. "Go with your lady!"

"B-b-but—" I stammer, trying to tell Frankie Bell that Daysha is just a classmate.

"No need to get all shook up, Moonie," Frankie Bell says. "Like I said, you done good!"

OMG, Frankie Bell, chill! I open my mouth to set him straight, but then the school's main door opens, and in walks Chris Carouthers and a camera guy! My mouth drops open. I mean, yeah, I emailed him and invited him, but a part of me didn't think he'd actually come! Frankie Bell 'bout to see that I'm definitely not ordinary anymore! I wave at Chris and he waves and smiles back.

But then, Chris stops smiling when he looks at something behind me. His eyes get real big, and he starts rushing toward me, fast. I turn around and freeze when I see what he's running toward.

It's Frankie Bell, toppling forward and crashing to the floor.

CHAPTER 23

"When it's my time, I wanna rest easy,
knowing all y'all have found
your path in life."

Mr. G drives me to the hospital, and his sister comes, too. She keeps turning around to ask if I'm okay or to let me know it's gonna be okay. I don't answer her on the first thing, and I don't believe her on the second.

In the hospital waiting room, I squeeze my eyes shut, but that's a mistake, because the only thing there is Frankie Bell hitting the ground with a *thwack!* and all the kids in the lobby gasping and Chris Carouthers dialing 911 on his cell phone.

I pop my eyes open and sit up. I called Aunt Kat from the school, but not my sister.

"Wh-what about Sh-Shannon?" I ask.

"Shannon?" Mr. G frowns.

"My s-s-sister. I n-need to c-c-call her," I tell him. Shannon needs to be here.

"No problem, you can use my phone," Mr. G says, handing me his cell. I go to the keypad but end up staring at the numbers. I *know* I know her number, but it's just not coming to me right now.

Luckily, it doesn't have to. Shannon and Ju rush into the waiting room a few seconds later and Shannon grabs me like I'm her kid.

"Xavier, you okay?"

"Y-y-yeah, b-but Frankie Bell." I can't get any more words out, plus, duh, Shannon knows Frankie Bell's not okay.

"Aunt Kat's here," Shannon tells me. "They let her go up to the surgery floor."

"Aight, l-let's go," I say.

"Nah, Xav, we gotta stay down here for a bit."

"Cuz he's dead."

I shock everyone with the words, but they're probably all thinking it.

"Xav, no, he's not!" Shannon's voice shakes, but the look she gives me is intense.

"He's not."

After a few minutes of silence, Mr. G introduces himself to Shannon.

"I can stay if you need me to," he tells her.

"No, we're okay," Shannon says. "Thank you for bringing Xavier from the dance."

"It was no problem at all; I'm here to help," Mr. G says.

He looks like he really doesn't want to leave, but after a few seconds he gives me dap and walks out the hospital with his sister, leaving me with mine.

Shannon taps away on her phone and groans.

"Ugh! Aunt Kat's so bad with her cell phone!" she says. "She ain't answering none of my texts!"

Shannon gets up and goes to the people at the main desk. I hear her say Frankie Bell's name and "ambulance," but I tune out the rest.

"You aight, Xav?" Ju asks me.

"Yeah."

"Hang in there, man," Ju says. "It's gonna be okay."

"Y-you d-d-d-don't know that," I tell him. "He could b-b-be d-dead."

"You right, man," Ju says, which surprises me. "But even if he is, like I said, it's gonna be aight. We're gonna be aight."

I think about that for a minute, both believing him and not believing him.

"She said somebody gonna come tell us something in a minute," Shannon says when she comes back. She sits and starts bouncing her leg up and down, like she does when she's nervous. A few minutes later, a guy in scrubs with the name tag DOUG B. walks over to us.

"Ms. Moon?" he asks.

"Yeah, that's me," Shannon says, standing up fast.

"Thank you for your patience, ma'am. Your uncle hit his head when he fell and was rushed to surgery upon his arrival. I can take you to that waiting room, and the doctors will be able to update you from there."

We follow Doug without a word down the twists and turns of the hospital hallways, and Aunt Kat's already in the second waiting room when we get there. When she looks up and sees us, there's a mix of fear and relief on her face.

"Shannon, thought I told y'all to just go on home. No use waitin' around here," Aunt Kat says. But when she hugs us, she holds on tight. She even hugs Ju!

"Julian, you didn't have to come here," Aunt Kat says, sinking into the chair she was sitting in.

"Yes, I did, Miz Kat," Ju says, and when he sits down right beside her, she doesn't give him a rude "get up from here!" look. Instead, she pats his knee and sighs.

"They say he had a stroke," she says. "And since that fool is diabetic, he went into a coma. I always told him he gotta take care of himself on the road! Hardheaded as always!"

It's like Aunt Kat can't decide whether to be sad or pissed off at her brother, which I kinda get. I mean, did Frankie Bell know he was having a stroke? What if he knew something wasn't right, but he still came to see me at my dance? He should've gone to the hospital, not to a stupid middle school! I slump forward until my head is almost on my knees. Few seconds later, I feel Shannon's hand on my back. I take a deep breath and start to tell her this is kinda my fault, but I don't get a chance to.

"Xav, shut up," Shannon cuts me off. "Shut *up*. It's okay. It's gonna be okay."

I guess everybody's obsessed with the word "okay."

"How was the dance, Moonie?" Aunt Kat asks. I think she's tryna take her mind off things, but that's not what it does for me. My heart tightens up when she uses the nickname Frankie Bell gave me.

"It w-was okay," I tell her. Might as well use the word, too.

"That's good. That's good." Aunt Kat nods. "You looked real nice when you went out the house."

It gets quiet again, and we all find boring things to stare at. I'm studying the patterns on the floor, looking for shapes or animals like on the ceiling in my room. I'm pretty sure I see Sonic the Hedgehog when a voice says, "Family of Frank Bell?" and I jump a little.

"That's us," Aunt Kat says. "You comin' with news or just to see if we need coffee? Cuz we don't need coffee."

"Ma'am, I'm Dr. Martin, and I assisted Dr. Howe during your brother's surgery. He did suffer a severe stroke and fell into a diabetic coma, but we were able to control the bleeding in his brain. The operation went as well as can be expected."

Dr. Martin explains that they'll be monitoring Frankie Bell closely and that his brain needs to rest. She asks if we have any questions, and Shannon rattles off a bunch. She's been Googling about strokes and comas ever since we got here. Mainly, Dr. Martin says a lot of things I don't understand and tells us they'll let us know when we can see Frankie Bell.

"Thank you, Dr. Martin," Aunt Kat says. "I'll be right here waitin' for your next update."

"You're very welcome, ma'am, but at this point, you might want to consider getting some rest," Dr. Martin says. "Mr. Bell is stable right now, and you likely won't be able to see him until much later anyway."

"I appreciate your suggestion, Doc, but I'll rest at the end of this, not the middle," Aunt Kat says. Dr. Martin nods like she hears people say this all the time, and she leaves us alone.

"Julian, I need for you to take them home," Aunt Kat says as soon as Dr. Martin is gone.

"Aunt Kat, that doctor is right; you should get some rest," Shannon says. "You and Xav go home. Me and Ju will stay."

"I said my piece, Shannon," Aunt Kat says. "I'm gonna be the first scowlin' face that fool sees when he wakes up."

"But, Aunt Kat, you don't need to be up here by yourself," Shannon counters. "I'll stay with you. Ju can take Xav home."

Aunt Kat gives Shannon a look.

"Who said I'll be by myself, little girl?" she says.

And right on cue, Mr. Alvin, Aunt Kat's "man-friend," glides into the waiting room.

"Well, I guess you won't be," Shannon says under her breath.

We all hug Aunt Kat goodbye, and Shannon tells her a million times to call us when Frankie Bell wakes up.

Nobody says much on the drive home; Ju doesn't even play music. Larmity is quiet at this time of night, and if it wasn't so cold, I'd go on a walk.

I get to the front door before Shannon and see a note taped to the screen. At first, I hold my breath, thinking there's *no way* this could be from Frankie Bell. I'm right; it's not. But it's still a good note.

Xavier, I hope everything's okay with your
uncle. The dance was really nice!
 —Daysha

Awww man! Everything happened so fast, I forgot all about Daysha, and I feel bad that she had to find her own way home. I'm also hoping Sole Crew did all right without me.

When we get inside, I don't even bother going to my room, and Shannon doesn't stop me when I open the basement door and head downstairs.

Everything looks exactly the same as last time, like he wasn't even here. His bed is made up perfectly—like, who *does* that? Aunt Kat says he's always been a neat freak. She also says he's neat in everything except his mind.

There's a hat on Frankie Bell's pillow, tan with a burgundy stripe around it. I walk closer and stare at the hat, then glance around the room, even though I know Frankie Bell's not gonna jump out and catch me snoopin'. *Stop trippin',* I tell myself. I reach down and pick up the hat. I was gonna put it on my head and see how I look. But instead, I immediately drop it like it's covered in Aunt Kat's hot oil for frying chicken.

There's a piece of paper on his pillow. A note.

With my name on it.

It takes me a few seconds before I even pick the note up. I'm being all dumb inside, imagining Frankie Bell watching me (somehow) and cracking up at how shook I am. I unfold the letter.

Moonie,

   I see we still enjoying special time in other people's personal spaces. I'll give you the benefit of the doubt and say that you're coming down here for inspiration, not to be nosy like your aunt. If I'm right, you're more than welcome. I learned long ago to linger round where greatness lives. Trust me, greatness ain't never far if you lookin' for it. Sometimes it's right beneath your feet.... Sometimes it's ON your feet, know what I'm sayin'? You come a long way, but don't get comfortable. Let's see what else you can do.
                                    —Frankie Bell

   I kick off my shoes, sit on Frankie Bell's bed, and read the note again and again, until my eyes start burning and I can't fight sleep anymore.

CHAPTER 24

*"No need to get all shook up,
Moonie."*

Shannon wakes me up early to say that Frankie Bell is still in a coma.

"C-can you m-m-mmmake waffles?"

It's the first thing I can think of to say, and even though Shannon gives me a look, I think she understands.

"Yeah," she says. "I'll make waffles and eggs."

"Nice."

When she goes upstairs, I sit up and look around for Frankie Bell's note. No way did it just vanish! Something tells me to check under the bed, and that's where I find it.

Man, Frankie Bell even keeps things neat under his bed! Who does that? Only a few pairs of old-man shoes lined up and a couple of suitcases. I put the note in my pocket and head for his closet. More old-man shoes and old-man clothes hanging up. In the corner is a red-and-white umbrella that looks like a peppermint, and on the top shelf are a bunch of shoeboxes that look like cool stuff might be in them. Maybe this is where he keeps his stacks of money. I grab the first one and open it to find a pair of *ladies'* shoes—red high heels.

What the?! I put that box up super quick and grab another one, which is stuffed with pictures. I sit crossed-legged on the rug by Frankie Bell's bed and go through them. I don't know many of the people, but some of the pictures are those old-school ones where you can write stuff on a white space at the bottom.

Oh snap! First picture is Frankie Bell in the tub with who I'm guessing are his sisters. He looks mad, but the girls are smiling. *Thelma, Marlene, and Frank, 1948* is what the writing at the bottom says. Ugh, it's like every parent has to do the naked bathtub pics!

There's another picture of four girls—*Kat, Dorothy, Thelma, and Marlene, 1954*—all dressed up for church and grinning big. Aunt Kat and her little sisters. She kinda looks the same, super serious and protective. I can't stop staring at the next picture I grab. *Arthur and Frank, 1962.* It's my grandfather and Frankie Bell, with their arms slung around each other's shoulders.

Brothers. They both have on hats like the one that was on Frankie Bell's bed. The photo's in black and white, but I think how crazy it would be if it's the same hat.

I make it through half of the pictures by the time Shannon calls me up to eat.

"L-look at this," I tell her, sliding the picture of Frankie Bell and our grandfather across the table.

"Oh wow, that's Granddad!" Shannon says with a grin. "You down there going through Frankie Bell's stuff?"

I take a huge bite of her homemade waffles instead of answering.

"Mmm-hmm, you know he don't like that," Shannon tells me. "Make sure you put everything back perfectly."

Shannon's eggs are salty and fluffy, just how I like them. I'm digging into a pile of them when the doorbell rings.

Shannon and I stare at each other, and then she narrows her eyes.

"If that's the aunts, somebody's gettin' slapped," she tells me, pushing up from the table. I hurry up and follow her to the door, cuz I really think she would slap one of our aunts, and I don't wanna miss it.

Shannon yanks the front door open, but it's not Aunt Nadine and Aunt Crys standing there. It's just Mr. Talbert, holding what looks like a cake.

"Good morning, young people, hope I didn't wake you," he says with a small smile. "Saw your uncle's car yesterday and wanted to bring him one of his favorites."

When me and Shannon don't say anything, Mr. Talbert clears his throat.

"He still in town?"

"Yeah, he is but . . ." Shannon pauses and opens the screen door. "Come in, Mr. Talbert."

"Everything all right?" Mr. Talbert asks, watching both of our faces.

"Not really," Shannon says with a sigh. "Frankie Bell had a stroke. My aunt just called and said he's still in a coma."

"Frankie?" Mr. Talbert gets a horrified look on his face and for a second it looks like he might pass out. He gives the cake to me and puts a hand on the doorframe for support.

"You need to sit down, Mr. Talbert?" Shannon asks.

"I—I was not expectin' that at all. Not at all," Mr. Talbert says, shaking his head. "I wouldn't even be making these cakes without your uncle, y'all know that?"

Me and Shannon shake our heads.

"Y-y-yyyou s-s-sssaid he wrote you letters," I say, remembering what Mr. Talbert said about the letters saving his life.

"He sho' did." Mr. Talbert nods. "After my CeeCee passed away, I was in bad shape. Didn't see a point in livin'. Here I was, switchin' to the night shift at the plant so I could spend more time with her, and the next thing I know, she's gone. Your uncle, he came around, tried to lift my spirits, but wasn't no lifting of anything right then. So he started writing me letters."

"What he say?" asks Shannon. I wonder if it was weird, cryptic stuff like what he writes me.

"All kinds of things," Mr. Talbert says with a smile. "But basically, he told me to do something I loved, and fast. Kept tellin' me the next time he came home I betta have a caramel cake waiting for him!"

Mr. Talbert laughs and points at the cake I'm holding.

"That's what you got in your hands, Xavier," Mr. Talbert says. "I made a cake for him way back then—my mama's recipe—and I been baking ever since. Turned it into a little side hustle."

Mr. Talbert tells us to let him know if there's anything we need and to keep him posted on how Frankie Bell's doing. He's halfway down the porch steps when Aunt Kat and Mr. Alvin pull into the driveway. Shannon stays at the door, probably waiting for Aunt Kat to come in so she can bombard her with questions, but I put the cake in the kitchen and head up to my room. I climb up onto my dresser and watch Mr. Talbert give Aunt Kat a hug and talk to her for a few minutes. I watch Mr. Talbert make his way slowly to his house and think about how Frankie Bell got him into baking. Seems like Frankie Bell's letters have helped a lot of people.

Maybe it's time he got some of his own.

CHAPTER 25

*"I learned long ago to linger round
where greatness lives."*

Despite a health incident with jazz legend, middle school fundraiser dance still a success!

CitySpeak has pictures of the dance on the front page, along with our donation bin. Turns out we collected almost a thousand pairs of socks. After he called 911 for Frankie Bell, Chris Carouthers stuck around and covered the story. Daysha shows me a clip from the news at least three times, probably because it's her and Tori who got interviewed.

My name and face are nowhere to be found.

"We should get these pictures framed," Alyssa says. She brought the paper to class and we spend the first fifteen minutes celebrating. Well, *they* spend most of class celebrating. I'm trying to smile and be happy, but I got a lot on my mind. Yeah, it sucks to see a picture of the Sole Crew without me in it, but it sucks even more to know that another day passed and Frankie Bell still hasn't woken up. I can tell Aunt Kat's getting more worried each day, which is probably why she's taking me and Shannon to see him today.

"Mrs. Clark, could we make T-shirts with this one?" Shyanne asks, pointing to the picture of the Sole Crew in front of the donation bin.

"It's a nice picture, but it's missing a member," Mrs. Clark says. "A founding member, at that. I think we can take a new picture."

"Oh. Yeah, you right," Shyanne says, glancing at me. Actually, everybody's eyes find their way over to me, and the moment is super awkward. It gets even worse when I hear my name over the intercom.

"Pardon the interruption. Xavier Moon to the main office. Xavier Moon to the main office, please."

I catch Mrs. Clark's eye when I stand up to leave and she looks as worried as I feel. Weird.

The halls are quiet, but I can feel the end-of-the-day buzz coming from the classrooms. Our dance flyer is still on the bulletin board by the office, and it feels like all that happened a million years ago. When I open the office door and don't see Aunt Kat or Shannon there, I breathe a sigh of relief.

"Hi, Xavier," Mrs. Miller says with a smile. "You can go on in. Mr. Roland is waiting for you."

I hear laughter coming from Mr. Roland's office, so I'm guessing things are okay. I knock on the half-open door, step inside, and see Mr. Roland . . . and Mr. Donnel?

"Mr. Moon, come on in," Mr. Roland says, gesturing to the seat by Mr. Donnel. "Have a seat. Judging by the shocked look on your face, I'm guessing you know my good friend Mr. Donnel."

"Umm, y-y-yeah," I say. At the last second, I remember to stretch out my hand to shake Mr. Donnel's. That's when I notice what's in his lap. A copy of today's *City-Speak.*

"How you doing today, young man?" Mr. Donnel asks.

"I'm g-good," I tell him. "H-how about you?"

"I'm fantastic!" Mr. Donnel says. "Always a pleasure to come back to my old stomping grounds and see my partner in crime runnin' things."

Mr. Roland and Mr. Donnel laugh again, like they're in on some kind of secret.

"Xavier, you're probably wondering why you were called down here, so I'll let Mr. Donnel take it away."

"I've been told you're the young man behind this."

Mr. Donnel holds up the paper, and I see the Sole Crew, minus one, grinning back at me.

"Y-yeah, k-kinda," I say.

"I read the story earlier this morning, and when I saw that kids at *my* middle school did this, I just had to come on over and investigate. Your principal tells me that not only did you start the Sole Crew, but that you also been bringing some serious sock game to Rosewood."

Mr. Donnel looks down at my feet, and I feel relieved that I put on some Frankie Bell socks today.

"So it looks like two things happened, Xavier," Mr. Donnel continues. "Number one, you listened to what I said last time we talked, and number two, I was wrong about you."

I'm not sure what Mr. Donnel means, but my heart's beating fast like something exciting is about to happen.

"Cut to the chase, Greg," Mr. Roland says. "Gotta get this young man back to class."

"Right," Mr. Donnel says. "Well, the bottom line is this. Your principal's recommendation carries a lot of weight, and he thinks you're League-ready. I told you before that it's rare for us to do a spring intake, but as you know, rare isn't impossible. If you're still interested, we'd like to induct you into the Scepter League in February."

I look back and forth from Mr. Donnel to Mr. Roland. Is this really happening? I'm getting into the League?

"Does that grin mean you're still interested?" Mr. Donnel asks.

"Y-yeah, of c-c-course I am!" I tell him. "Th-thank you!"

"Don't thank me, young man. You did all the work," Mr. Donnel says, shaking my hand again. "We'll be in touch about February."

"Good job, Xavier," Mr. Roland says. "Glad to have you in the League."

"W-wait, y-you were in the L-L-League, too?" I ask.

"What, you can't tell?" Mr. Roland pops his collar.

"You must be gettin' old," Mr. Donnel jokes.

"I only get better with time," Mr. Roland says. "And speaking of time, Xavier, you can head to class. Congratulations again."

As I'm walking down the hall, the first thing I think is that Frankie Bell and my dad are gonna go ballistic when I tell them. And that's when it hits me that I won't be able to tell either one of them, at least not right away. It's funny how one second I'm so excited about something, and the next second I forget all about the good news. I finally got everything I wanted, but now it doesn't even matter.

CHAPTER 26

*"Trust me, greatness ain't never far if
you lookin' for it."*

Hospital rooms freak me out.

They're cold and quiet and beep-y, and I don't wanna move at all because it feels like if I step the wrong way, I'll knock something over and end up flatlining somebody. Shannon keeps nudging me forward from the spot in the doorway where I'm standing frozen, and I'm legit trippin' out.

"Xav, go stand by the bed. It's cool," she says.

I'm staring at the bed and I see cords and tubes and machines, and nah. I'm good at the door.

"Boy, if you don't get in this room!" Aunt Kat hisses cuz we're supposed to keep our voices down, and her "nudge" is a little bit stronger than Shannon's. I stumble forward but keep my balance as I get closer to the bed.

Frankie Bell's perfectly still, and he reminds me of a tree—big and strong, with the tubes coming out of him like branches. I cringe when I see the tube going down his throat, breathing for him.

"D-does he f-f-feel that?" I whisper to Shannon. She stares at the machine and its noises before shrugging.

"He ain't gonna jump up and bite you," Aunt Kat says. "Y'all get closer and say your piece."

Shannon moves up near Frankie Bell's head and tells him she loves him and misses him.

"Me and Ju been listenin' to your music," Shannon says. "Not gonna lie; *Smooth Distance* and *Heaven's Eleven* go hard."

Wait a second. *Heaven's Eleven?* That's what Mrs. Clark's always calling our class. I wonder if she listens to Frankie Bell's music, too. Shannon tells Frankie Bell what she made for dinner last night, and what recipe she's gonna try next, but I keep thinking about that phrase. *Heaven's Eleven.* When it gets quiet again, I don't have to look up to know that Aunt Kat and Shannon are staring at me, telling me with their eyes and head motions that it's my turn to talk. I swallow hard. Open and close my mouth. Twice. I know exactly what I wanna do, but it feels weird to do it with Shannon and Aunt Kat in here.

"C-c-ccccan I t-t-tttalk to him alone?" I ask.

At first, a frown crosses Aunt Kat's face and it looks like she might whisper-cuss me out. But then she nods and motions for Shannon to follow her out the room.

I listen to the whirs and beeps of the machines for a while, and it's really hypnotizing. No wonder Frankie Bell's still asleep. I bet if they started playing his jazz music in here, he'd wake up real quick.

I take a step closer and stare at Frankie Bell's face. I feel like his eyes are gonna pop open any second, which would be cool, but would also scare the crap outta me. I wonder if anything hurts, and he's lying there and can't tell anybody. I wonder if he knows I'm here.

Don't just stand there like a pillar of salt, Moonie; get on with it!

I flinch and glance around the room, then at Frankie Bell, cuz I *swear* I heard his voice. He hasn't moved, though, and the machines are still doing their thing. I reach in my pocket and pull out a piece of paper. My letter.

Frankie Bell,

It was really cool that you came to my dance, but maybe you shouldn't have. Maybe Aunt Kat's been right all this time, and you shoulda just sat your old self down somewhere. (Her words, not mine.) But

I get it. You love your music. I've learned a lot about you that I didn't know before, from your letters and from looking through all the stuff in your room downstairs. I been sleeping down there every night, by the way. (If you're mad about that, you gotta wake up and tell me.) At first it was kinda creepy, and I had to sleep with the bathroom light on. But then I got used to it. Anyway, since you like writing weird letters to people, I thought I'd write one to you. So here's the thing. I got some great news today, and I really wanna tell you. But you gotta wake up first. That's the deal. And a man who don't keep a deal ain't a man.

So wake up.

—Moonie

P.S. Tell the nurse to get you something else to wear. This gown looks ugly on you.

It takes me a while to read the letter out loud, and I keep thinking Shannon and Aunt Kat or a nurse will bust in the room when I'm right in the middle of it. But I finish reading, fold the letter up, and slip it under the blanket near Frankie Bell's hand. I sit in the chair by his bed and listen for a crackling noise over the sound of the machines.

"Xavier, you done playing around?" Aunt Kat says, coming into the room. "Frankie's got another visitor."

There's a lady behind Aunt Kat, and I don't see who it is until Aunt Kat moves to the side.

Mrs. Clark??

"Wh-what are y-you d-d-doing here?" I ask.

"Well, hello to you, too, Mr. Moon," Mrs. Clark says. "I'm here to say hello to a very dear friend."

"M-m-me?" There should be a limit on the number of weird things that can happen in a day.

"Boy, what's wrong with you?" Aunt Kat says, half laughing, half fussing. "She's here to see your uncle!"

Okay. I'm officially confused. How does Mrs. Clark know Frankie Bell? Maybe she's a fan of his music?

"I been knowing your uncle for years! Back in Bell-Aires' heyday, I was the group's costume designer; kept them sharp from head to toe," Mrs. Clark says, answering my question before I can ask it. "Small world, isn't it?"

I'm too busy thinking to respond. So *that's* why Mrs. Clark kept saying "heaven's eleven"! Man, Frankie Bell really does have eyes everywhere! Mrs. Clark's probably one of his spies, letting him know my every move at school.

"You okay, Xavier?" Mrs. Clark asks.

"Umm, y-yeah," I say, my mind still racing.

"Gloria, we gonna give you some privacy with him," Aunt Kat says, patting Mrs. Clark's arm.

"Oh, you know that's not necessary, Kat," Mrs. Clark protests.

"Naw, you go on ahead. My kitchen ain't seen me in three days, and it's calling my name right now," Aunt Kat says. The two of them hug tight before we leave, which makes me think they've known each other a loooonng time.

When we get home, Aunt Kat goes straight to the kitchen and I head right to the basement. I open Frankie Bell's closet and look through more of his pictures. I find one that says *Frank in Europe,* and it must've been taken in the winter, because he has on a coat and scarf. Frankie Bell's wearing his usual fedora and he's sitting at a piano, hands on the keys and a cigar in his mouth. He's leaning forward slightly and I'm guessing he was really playing, not just posing. When I look closer at the scarf around Frankie Bell's neck, I get an idea. I leave all the pictures scattered on the floor and start rummaging through the closet. I've seen that scarf before. It's a wild thought, but I know exactly what to do if I can find it.

I go through Frankie Bell's closet, his dresser drawers, and every box under his bed. No scarf, *and* he's gonna be pissed when he comes down here and sees his room.

I'm about to give up when I remember the box with the red shoes.

I open the box, and bingo! There's the scarf folded neatly underneath the shoes.

It's a black-and-white scarf and the designs on it remind me of piano keys, which is probably why Frankie Bell still has it after all these years. It's soft and scratchy at the same time, but I think it'll work.

I put the scarf in my bookbag, and for the first time ever, I can't wait to get to sewing class.

CHAPTER 27

"You come a long way, but don't get comfortable."

"**H**ow's he doing?"

Mr. Talbert's face is twisted up in worry this morning at the bus stop.

"S-s-ssstill asleep," I say. "We g-g-gggoing to s-see him today."

Mr. Talbert nods and hands me a peppermint.

"I sho' am hopin' and prayin' he comes around," he says. I'm hoping that, too.

On the bus, Daysha sits by me and grins.

"Wanna hear some good news?" she asks.

"You m-m-mmmade the t-team?"

Daysha nods. "It's official. Eighth-grade team."

"I m-mean, w-we all kn-knew that was gonna h-h-hhhhappen," I tell her.

"Yeah," Daysha says. "Just like I know your uncle's gonna get better."

And for some reason, when she says it, I believe her.

At school, when I'm putting my coat in my locker, someone runs up behind me and grabs my shoulders.

"Yoooo! Heard you gettin' in the League, boiiii!"

Latrell.

I grin and give him dap.

"That's wassup!" Latrell says. "You know when your induction ceremony is?"

"Nah," I say. "M-Mr. Donnel h-hasn't t-t-ttttold me."

"Yo, mine was fiyah!" Latrell says. "My dad was, like, teary and whatnot."

Latrell goes on and on about how the ceremony was long and low-key boring, but that it was super cool to get his Scepter League jacket, and his dad took him and his friends out to eat at a fancy restaurant after.

"I'm for real; dude dropped like two hundred dollars!"

Me and Latrell are walking to Innovation Lab now, and I'm thinking about my initiation day and who I'd want to be there. If Frankie Bell was okay, I bet he'd take me out to eat, too.

I'm nervous about the end of the day, when I get to see him again. It's day three of him being in a coma, and

I know he can't stay like that forever, stuck in the hospital with machines breathing for him.

When Aunt Kat picks me up from school, Shannon's already in the car with her. The ride to the hospital is quiet, and it's, like, the first time Aunt Kat drives without almost hitting something. I feel like those two know something and aren't telling me, but I'm too scared to ask.

Frankie Bell looks exactly the same as last time and I wonder if he's bored just lying there.

"Brought Shannon and Moonie again to see you, Frankie," Aunt Kat tells her brother. "Cold outside; might have some snow comin' our way."

"I'm makin' my famous chili tonight," Shannon says. "Xav probably gonna punk out cuz he thinks it's too spicy."

"Whatever." I roll my eyes. Frankie Bell should know by now that I'm definitely not no punk. After Shannon and Aunt Kat finish with all their small talk, I'm ready to get down to real man business.

"I n-n-. . . nnnneed to t-talk to him alone," I say.

"Dang, Xav, you gonna do this all the time?" Shannon asks.

"Just leave it be, girl," Aunt Kat says, surprising me again. She does add a zinger under her breath on the way out, though: "Two peas in a twisted pod."

Once they're gone and it's quiet, except for the

beeps and whirs, I drop my bookbag on the chair next to Frankie Bell, reach into my pocket for my next letter, and start reading out loud.

> Frankie Bell,
>   You're not holding up your end of the deal, which is pretty messed up. Means I can't tell you my news, which is real real REAL good news. So what's your plan? To just lay around and miss everything? Let some other group take over the "old-man music" industry? Or are you gonna be like me and wake up and do something? Sometimes the answer is right at your toes.
>   —Moonie

I tuck the letter by his hand like last time and notice that the first one isn't there anymore. Nurses probably moved it, which is pretty rude if you ask me, but I don't have time to get all upset off of that. I unzip my bookbag and pull out the present I have for Frankie Bell.

"You st-still in the s-s-s-sssame ugly gown," I tell Frankie Bell, shaking my head like he sees me. I walk to the end of the bed and untuck all the sheets and blankets, careful not to bump anything. It feels weird to see Frankie Bell's big old feet with nothing on them. It feels even weirder to slide on the socks I made for him.

I hope he won't get mad, but I made the socks out of that black-and-white piano scarf. Mrs. Clark let me use a sewing machine yesterday after school, and it was actually kinda fun. When I first showed Mrs. Clark the scarf, she held it and smiled.

"I have a real good memory, especially when it comes to clothes. I picked this out for him when we were overseas performing. He wore it at one of his first integrated shows here in the states."

Since Mrs. Clark was the one who had bought the scarf and actually liked my sock idea, I didn't feel so bad cutting it.

"You the v-very f-first person to w-w-wear my line of s-s-ssssocks," I tell Frankie Bell. "Design n-number one."

I bet Frankie Bell's feet are feelin' nice and warm now. I find out for sure when I'm about to tuck the covers back and I see his right foot move, just a tiny bit.

"Frankie Bell! You just moved!" I say, louder than I should have. I stare at his feet, and this time the toes on his right foot jerk slightly. I stare at his face, and even though his eyes stay shut, his cheek twitches.

"Frankie Bell, the s-sock company isn't m-my b-big news," I say. I tell him I made it into the Scepter League, that they're gonna do a spring initiation, mainly because of me. And I tell him exactly what I told Mr. Donnel yesterday.

That I can wait.

"I'm n-n-not g-gonna do it till y-you can be there," I say. I tell him to hurry up and get better so I can get that green and gold.

"You done botherin' your uncle with these secret sessions?" Aunt Kat says when she comes in.

"He m-moved, Aunt Kat!" I tell her. She looks from me to him, sees the socks on his feet.

"Lord have mercy, whatchoo do, Moonie, put a sock spell on him?" she asks, going closer to look at his face.

"M-maybe it *was* the s-s-socks, Aunt Kat," I say. Frankie Bell flicks his toes again and Aunt Kat forgets all about her rule of being quiet and goes off thanking Jesus and hollering for the nurse.

We stay at the hospital for a long time, even after they tell us for the third time that visiting hours are over. The nurses say that even though Frankie Bell moving is a step in the right direction, he still has a long road ahead of him.

"Well, we appreciate you sayin' that," Aunt Kat says. "But that man there was born on the road, and one more trip ain't gonna scare him."

It doesn't happen often, but Aunt Kat finally says the right thing at the right time.

EPILOGUE

"Moonie, you are the swag now."

"Lawd, that fool done opened his eyes!"

I hear Aunt Kat from all the way up in my room, and I immediately dash downstairs.

It's a few days before Christmas break starts and both me and Shannon are busy doing our things. She's in the kitchen whipping up some bananas Foster pancakes, and I've been up in my room, busy with the early Christmas gift I got from Mrs. Clark. I swear, I never thought I'd be excited to see a sewing machine, but when Mrs. Clark and her son brought it over a few days ago, I wanted to set it up right away. I moved my dresser over a little, so the sewing machine sits right in front of my window. Perfect place for me to make socks for my business, Socks from the Block. After I made Frankie Bell's socks,

I started making more as Christmas gifts. I even have pairs for Ma and Dad, which I'm hoping I can give them in person.

When I get down to the kitchen, Aunt Kat still has her coat on and there's a relieved smile on her face.

"H-h-he's awake?" I ask.

"Just for a few minutes," Aunt Kat says. "Long enough to see my face and know I mean business about him turnin' the corner on this thing!"

Me and Shannon laugh. If Frankie Bell was here laughing with us, he'd probably say something like, "Moonie, yo' aunt Kat's face made me wanna go on back to sleep!" I can already hear it.

"Can we see him?" Shannon asks.

"Why you think I'm here, lil' girl?" Aunt Kat laughs and swats Shannon's arm.

"Course, you got it smellin' so good in this kitchen, we gon' have to take care of business first."

While we eat, Aunt Kat tells us about all the therapy Frankie Bell will have to do to get back to normal. The nurses say he'll have to learn to walk and talk again, and that he'll probably have a speech teacher just like me.

"He'll probably get somebody like that one-letter man from your school," Aunt Kat says with a grunt. Now, *that* would be funny! Frankie Bell and Mr. G would probably get along just fine.

I'm stuffing a sweet bite of pancake into my mouth when the doorbell rings.

"Okay, this is getting old," Shannon says. But I know it's not my aunts by the way the bell keeps ringing and ringing. Only one person would do that.

"Hey, W-Walter," I say when I answer the door. It's pretty cold out, but Walter barely has his coat on. He's all grins, holding up a box for me to see.

"Look, look! I made you something!" he shouts. "Can I show Mrs. Aunt Kat?"

I open the door and he scoots inside, calling for Aunt Kat as if he knows her like that.

"Mrs. Aunt Kat, look! I made you something! Remember you said your favorite thing is gardening? Open it, open it!" Walter sticks the box way too close to Aunt Kat's face and she leans away and frowns.

"Well, how am I gonna open it if it's up my nose?" she asks.

"Sorry!" Walter laughs. He bounces from foot to foot as Aunt Kat opens the box and pulls out an ornament.

"It's a garden!" Walter exclaims.

Okay, not gonna lie. The ornament is low-key hideous. There's lots of brown and green and little dots of orange and red that I'm guessing are supposed to be vegetables. Aunt Kat squints as she looks at it and I know she's probably about to say something toxic.

But she doesn't.

"Well, this is just perfect for my tree," she tells him. Me and Walter both study her face, and she looks like she means it!

"You really like it? The kids on the bus said it's a hot mess." Walter looks super bummed when he says this, and he's *never* down.

"And when did you start caring about what kids on the bus say?" Aunt Kat says, waving her hand. "This is going right on my tree, and that's that!"

Walter nods, but his face still looks a little sad. I don't know why it's messin' with me so much, but it is. So I decide to do something about it.

"W-Walter, I g-g-got something for you, too," I say. I motion for him to follow me up to my room.

"Whoa, what's that?" Walter says, running up to my sewing machine.

"Yo, c-careful," I tell him right before he touches it. "That's where I m-m-mmmake magic."

"Whoa!" Walter says in a whisper. My plan is working; he's perking up. I hand him a pair of black-and-orange-striped socks that I made out of a blanket.

"This is so cool!" Walter says, bouncing up and down. "Tigers are my favorite!"

He kicks off his boots and pulls the socks on over the ones he's wearing.

"I'm gonna wear these every day!" Walter says. "Then I'll be cool, like you!"

"Nah," I tell him. "You already c-c-cool l-like you."

Walter grins and I think about the last line in the Scepter League Creed: *I will be a man who lights the way for others.* Maybe Walter can come to my induction ceremony, too.

"Look, Xavier, I got swwwwaaaag!" Walter says, doing a funky-looking spin move in his socks and pointing at me.

"Yeah." I grin, pointing back. "You got swag."

ACKNOWLEDGMENTS

My father had a speech impediment when he was young, and he's told us many stories of how it impacted him as a Black boy growing up in the South. Though nowhere near as severe, when I was a little girl, I struggled with my *l* and *y* sounds. If you didn't notice, those letters make up more than half my name! My older sister, Kim, would come to my rescue time and time again, telling people that my name wasn't "Katie," as it sounded when I pronounced it. Often frustrated, I would turn to my sister and say, "Tell them, Kim!" Kim's response was always clear: "Her name is *Kelly.*" Perhaps it is these memories, or the memories of our father's stories, that motivated my sister to choose speech pathology as a career. I watched her work diligently through both undergraduate and graduate school, and I see the discipline, preparation, and professionalism with which she serves. Kim, you were not only my first friend but my voice for a good minute! I am so proud of you! Thank you for sharing the tips, details, resources, and inside look at your world. Thanks for marrying a Kobe Lover! And of course, thanks for sayin' my name! Love is love!

To my parents, your support is priceless! I get so much joy from the thought of making you proud! To my sisters, thank you for having Facebook pages when I don't! ☺ I'm convinced that no one goes hard for you like your sisters! To my children . . . whew! Y'all make this thing hard! Which makes me Beast Mode for being able to do it! You five are my greatest chapters!

To my nephew, Xavier, thanks, man, for letting me snatch your name! ☺

To my ACA family, we truly lead the way! Thanks for always welcoming me with open arms. 18 to 1, did I cross yet? ☺

To Ora Sanders, when I first saw you, I immediately said, "There's Aunt Kat!" I had your face in mind as I wrote! To Sharonda Pearson, you are a witness to my previous statement! Thanks for the picture of your dad to serve as my Frankie Bell inspiration!

To my agent extraordinaire, Hannah Mann, we are such a great match! Thank you for your persistence and your belief in my words. Don't worry; Rose is coming! ☺

To Phoebe Yeh, Elizabeth Stranahan, and my Crown family, thank you for supporting the dreams that are embedded in each of my stories and for rolling up your sleeves to help me tackle the work that comes after *The End*.

To my readers, what is your *thing*? Once you discover what it is, pursue it with everything you got! A wise writer friend shared this quote with me: "You will have either the pain of discipline or the pain of regret." Be disciplined! Dream BIG, but wake up and WORK! Like the great Kobe Bryant, leave nothing on the court, the table, the easel, the laptop, the field, the studio. And as you do that, remember . . . true swag is in the socks! ☺

ABOUT THE AUTHOR

KELLY J. BAPTIST is the inaugural winner of the We Need Diverse Books short-story contest. Her story is featured in the WNDB anthology *Flying Lessons & Other Stories* and inspired her first full-length novel, *Isaiah Dunn Is My Hero.* Kelly is also the author of the picture book *The Electric Slide and Kai. The Swag Is in the Socks* was inspired by Kelly's love of unique and creative socks, as well as her older sister's hero work as a speech-language pathologist. When she's not writing, Kelly is usually thinking about writing . . . and dreaming of palm trees while living in southwest Michigan. She keeps beyond busy with her five amazing children, who always give her plenty of story ideas and background noise to write to. You can find Kelly online at kellyiswrite.com and on Twitter.